DISINHERITED

Son of a Millwright

Anne Mason

To my family and friends: without their support I may not have finished.

1

'Ma's at the door!' exclaimed William. That in itself was odd: usually she would be inside cooking because they always returned home from work hungry. As they came closer Henry could see that his mother's face was wet and her eyes red and swollen. Mary-Ann Spandler was crying. He'd never seen her shed a tear before and she was sobbing. He went to her, but she turned and went indoors.

The other children stared as they entered; but for the grizzling of three-month-old Martha it was quiet.

'What's happened? Pa? Is he hurt?' William questioned: his father worked in the family's millwrights' yard and it was often dangerous. Mary-Ann ignored him; she walked over to the shelf above the fire and turned back to Henry with a letter in her hand. Without looking up she handed it to him.

As he opened it his eyes narrowed; his frown deepened but his hands did not shake because, until the moment he read the words, he expected it to be simple.

'London!' he exclaimed. 'London!' His shoulders slumped. 'He's gone to London,' he repeated to himself as he shook his head.

'Why? Why? What does it mean?' William was trying to look over his shoulder.

'And he's sold his share of the yard.' Henry extruded the words from between clenched teeth.

'No!' William ran his hand through his hair. The front door opened and their sisters walked in. They stood still.

'What's happening? Where's Pa?' Eliza and Mary both asked together.

'He says he's gone to London and will come back a rich man before Christmas. I'm to look after Ma and you all until then.' Henry's voice was brittle and his eyes, wide and staring, scanned the room.

'Sold the yard! Sold the yard!' William repeated himself as he tried to comprehend. Eliza snatched off her bonnet and went to her mother. Mary-Ann was swaying. Eliza and Mary pulled her down onto the bed between them.

'He's gone,' she whined. 'Gone. I want him to come back.'

Henry looked again at the letter although he knew what it said. 'He says he will. At Christmas.' He looked at his mother who, for the first time since he'd come home, held his gaze. Tears flooded her face. He shuddered.

At twenty, Eliza was Henry's elder by two years; Mary was two years younger than him. As the oldest girls they prepared the food for the family that evening. Eliza took a small piece of potato and carrot from the pan that was boiling on the fire, mashed them with some of the oils that had leaked out of the fish. She tried to feed this to the baby, but Martha choked at first until Mary suggested adding some of the liquid from the pan to make it less solid. She managed to get her to take a little and then put some sugar in her rag and tied it up. Martha sucked on the sweetness and soon fell asleep. The rest of the family sat up at the table and ate, with the exception of their mother, Mary-Ann, who didn't eat but remained curled up on the bed. She was not asleep because her eyes were wide open: they flicked from one to another of her many children. Later the baby woke again and Mary persuaded her mother to feed her. She sat up and leant against Mary as if all her bones had been removed whilst Eliza held her baby to her nipple.

'Martha didn't drink much. I think Ma's milk is drying up,' Eliza said when all the younger children were upstairs asleep.

'It must be the shock,' suggested Mary.

'No,' said a small voice from the bed. Mary-Ann roused herself into a sitting position. 'It always happens when there is another baby growing.'

'What! You mean...?' Mary stared at her mother who nodded and flopped back down on the bed.

'I told him,' she whimpered, 'I told him, but he still had to go. Why? Why has he gone?'

Henry's grandfather had been the owner and master-in-charge of the family's millwrights' yard. Since his death three years ago the yard had been owned by Henry's father and his brothers, with his father, as the oldest, being the master-in-charge. In the confines of the yard was a large cottage where Henry's grandparents had lived and had brought up their family and which his grandmother had continued to occupy since the death of her husband until, last month, she'd followed him to the grave. The front room of the cottage was the office where the men collected their wages each week. In contrast, Henry's family lived in Garrison Walk. The town of Great Yarmouth took all of its noxious rubbish by cart past where they lived and deposited it on the bank of the River Bure. It was transported to farms along the river but the piles grew faster than they could be shovelled onto the boats: the stench was part of their lives. Henry and his family had always expected that, when his grandmother died, they would move into the cottage at the yard because his father was the master-in-charge.

A few days after his father left, Robert and James, Henry's uncles, called him into the office. It was much as Henry remembered it from visits to his grandparents although today men were moving past the office door with pieces of furniture. His attention was caught by the glass on the mantlepiece. It was a rummer, six inches high, its ovoid bowl engraved with a picture of a windmill and the words 'Thomas Spandler 1815'. It had been presented to his grandfather upon the completion of High Mill in Southtown and Henry remembered his first day at work when he was invited into the office to be shown it.

'We've decided that my family will move in here.' As Robert spoke Henry turned his attention to him. His words precipitated anger towards his father: now his family would stay at Garrison Walk. 'That must be hard I know,' Robert continued. Henry forced himself to concentrate on what he was saying. 'However, it's not the reason I asked you to come in here. I am increasing your wage.'

Henry raised his eyebrows. 'Did Pa ask you to do that? Did you know?'

'I knew he was going. James and I told him not to, but he wouldn't listen. Because he has gone and we don't know when – or even if – he will return, I am now master-in-charge.' Henry's face reddened as he struggled to control his anger. 'But no, your father did not ask any special favours of me and I tell you I'm only doing this for the sake of the yard. You are invaluable to me because you operate the engine so well. I have decided that your apprenticeship will soon be complete.'

'Soon! I thought that wouldn't be until two years come Christmas.'

'You're so quick at learning – but nevertheless that's how it would have been had your grandfather still been alive. In those days James and I thought that, before the end of seven years, we'd have to start making things up to teach you! But we're not going to do that. Times are changing and we need to adapt. When we've taught you what we know you'll be a millwright – whenever that is – we'll not be tied by the old system.'

'And we don't want you thinking that you need to earn more money and go looking for work elsewhere!' James interjected. 'When you're qualified we'll raise your wage again.'

'I'm pleased that you both value me so highly'. He stopped and looked at both his uncles in turn, 'but why did you not warn me my father was going?'

'I could not break my word to him. He's our brother,' Robert looked at James before turning back to meet Henry's eyes. 'He made us promise.'

'And what do you think are the chances of him returning?' Henry held his gaze.

Robert smiled. 'Be optimistic Henry. He may make his fortune.'

'Or not,' added James. 'Be realistic as well, because there's much that could go wrong for him. Your task is hard enough so put him out of your mind. You cannot help him.'

'He has crushed my mother. In the weeks since Grandmother's death she had been so excited at the thought of moving in here as the wife of the master-in-charge. Now she cries all the time and nothing Eliza and Mary can do seems to help.'

'The other children?'

'I thought we might have to send Caroline and Hannah to work and keep Rachel and Sarah at home but with this increase in my wage they should all be able to stay at school.' He smiled briefly. 'They're quiet and look frightened all the time although the little ones don't really know what's happened. There's not been much laughter the last few days.' He paused. 'Oh, and Eliza and Mary are worried about baby Martha. Ma has another baby in her and her milk is waning.'

'I'll ask Hannah,' James suggested. 'Our William is still taking from her and if she thinks it will not harm my son the baby could come to us for a few months and feed from her until she is fully weaned.'

'Thank you, Uncle James.'

'You no longer need to address us as uncle.' James looked at Robert who nodded. 'It's unnecessary. You're a man now.' Henry nodded but he did not smile. If someone had said that to him a week ago it would have delighted him. Now the words drilled into his head as he left the cottage: he had suddenly become a man with a man's responsibilities, it was hard and he felt inadequate.

He reached the end of the yard where the stationary steam engine stood and where the ironworks took place. The furnace that melted the iron was a complicated structure, designed to reach high temperatures, and was carefully managed so that the fire never went out. Adjacent to it, and connected by a chamber, was a smaller furnace which heated the boiler to power the steam engine. The proximity of the smaller furnace meant that, although it was extinguished each evening, it never went completely cold. Each morning fire was moved through the connecting chamber enabling the steam in the boiler to be quickly brought up to pressure to power the engine which drove many of the tools in the yard. Henry's skill in operating it kept the yard productive and it was this skill which Robert valued.

'William. Edmund. Come and see this,' he called to his brother and cousin who were apprentices. 'Look at that pressure. It's too high. When I'm not here and they're building up the heat on their side of the furnace you must keep a watch on it.'

'Keep watch yourself,' retorted Edmund. 'Where have you been anyway?'

'Talking to your father. This is important.' Henry pointed to the dial as Edmund raised his eyes. 'It could explode if the pressure valve is not released,' insisted Henry.

Edmund laughed. 'You're like an old woman. Always worrying about what might happen.'

'Did you not hear about Peterson's foundry? Three men were killed when their boiler burst.'

'That was a huge boiler. Not like this toy.' Edmund jabbed a finger at the steam engine.

'It is not a toy, Edmund. You need to learn.'

Suddenly there was a shout from the sand pit where iron was being poured into moulds. One of the other apprentices had tried to move the ladle containing molten metal but it had caught on the side on the pit and had spilt.

'Hold it steady Robert,' called James to the apprentice. 'The ladle is still dangerous even though the metal's gone.' The young man, his eyes wide, stood still. 'Now turn slowly and put the ladle down.' His hands shook but he managed to seat it safely in its cradle. 'Well done,' continued James, 'you stayed calm. We'll need to start again but that's as it is. At least no-one was hurt.'

Edmund, who along with everyone else in the yard had heard what had happened, guffawed. 'My clumsy brother again,' he shouted.

'Edmund your opinion was not asked for,' pronounced James.

'He's always breaking things at home as well,' continued Edmund as if James had not spoken.

'Edmund you are the youngest apprentice here. I heard Henry trying to instruct you about the engine and you weren't listening to him either.' James's voice was raised. He looked up to see his brother striding out of the cottage in their direction.

'What's happening here then?' Robert asked as he approached.

'It's our Rob being fumble-fisted again,' explained Edmund before James could say anything.

'Edmund!' James flicked his eyes between his brother and his nephew. 'Your younger son, our newest apprentice, seems to think he's as important as his father.'

'Which he is not,' said Robert with a look at Edmund. He turned to the pit where his eldest son, Robert, was raking in the pieces of metal that had by now solidified. 'But what do we have here? A morning's work wasted again?' The young Robert cringed whilst Edmund turned away. He was smirking. Henry looked at his two uncles and wondered if they were having the same thought that he was: if Henry's father did not return then young Robert would eventually become master-in-charge of Spandler's millwrights' yard.

That evening there was a knock at the door of the cottage in Garrison Walk. Eliza answered while Mary stood behind her holding Martha.

'Hello, Aunt Hannah. Henry told us you might call. Come in.'

'Let me see the child. Is she well? She has no disease?' Mary shook her head as she held Martha towards her aunt for inspection.

'She cries a lot but Ma does not hold her even when she tries to feed. I have to hold her up to the nipple but there's not much milk.' Hannah turned to Mary-Ann who was sitting in the rocking-chair by the fire.

'Come now Mary-Ann,' she coaxed. 'It's hard, I know, but you have children who need you.'

'How can you know?' Mary-Ann pouted, tears appearing in her eyes. 'I am bereft and my children have no father.'

'Your older children are caring for their siblings.'

'But I am on my own. I wait for them to come home each day.' She sighed and said under her breath, 'I wait for him to come but he doesn't.' Hannah heard her.

'But your older children come home,' she admonished, 'and they need you to care for the younger ones. What about your baby? You have no milk?'

'I carry another, so it has stopped.'

'Shall I take her home with me? I have plenty.' Mary-Ann looked to be about to object but then she flopped back into the chair. 'Are you eating?' Hannah continued, 'if you are carrying another you must.' Mary-Ann shrugged her shoulders. 'Your baby may die inside you if you don't and you will become ill.'

'The baby would be better off dead,' intoned Mary-Ann. 'It has no father.' Eliza and Mary gasped. Hannah tried to put her arm around Mary-Ann but she was repulsed.

'I'll take the baby home,' Hannah said, her eyes flicking between the two girls and their mother who was gripping the arms of the chair tightly and rocking. She took Martha from Eliza and left.

Later, when the younger children had been put to bed, Eliza, Henry, Mary and William sat together on the bench.

'I think we need to work this out between us,' Eliza said, 'at least until Ma has regained her wits.' Mary-Ann was still sitting in the rocking chair, agitating it with her foot whilst she stared at the floor; occasionally she looked up but only to glance at the front door to the cottage.

'These last few days have been hard,' Henry said.

'Yes,' agreed Mary, 'especially at the end of the day. We get home and they are all hungry. I don't think Ma is preparing food during the day.'

'I don't think she is doing anything,' added Eliza, 'judging by the smell when we came in. Elizabeth must sit all day in her own mess.' Mary-Ann continued to rock as if no-one was there. 'I think Ma is like this all the time.'

'Caroline said that when they came back from school in the middle of the day she found some bread and they had that and went back.' Mary looked thoughtful. 'There is soup at the school – rather thin and Ma always insisted we came home for something good to eat – but it's provided and I think Hannah, Rachel and Sarah can have that. If Caroline comes home without them she'll have time to feed Tom and Elizabeth while she eats.'

'Why don't we ask at Grout's if I could start work later and then I could go to the market,' suggested Mary. 'I'd need to work later at night though.'

'And if I start early,' added Eliza, 'I could finish early and call in at the market on my way home. Whatever's for sale then will be what's left over and won't be at its best but I should be able to buy cheaper for that.'

'What will they say at Grout's though?' William asked.

Eliza and Mary worked at Grout's silk factory. The factory had been destroyed by fire earlier that year but Eliza and Mary worked in a small corner of the old factory which was still standing. Boards had been put up to shield them from the dust whilst a new factory was built around them. Although they were girls they had also inherited the Spandler intelligence and dexterity. The management at Grout's recognised that they were part of a small group which had the resourcefulness to produce some silk in the difficult conditions. Their wages had been cut but it was better than losing the work altogether and they had been promised special positions in the new factory when it opened before the end of the year.

'There is so little room that they've been asking us to try to come in at different times. I'm sure they'll be pleased. It will be better for them and us,' said Eliza.

'I think you girls are wonderful!' William exclaimed.

'Yes,' agreed Henry, 'but remember that we do not have Pa's wage any more. Even with the increase that Robert has given me we have to live more poorly than we are used to.

2

As the months went by, the nights grew longer and Christmas approached. Henry's optimism rose. His family were coping with the circumstances in which his father had left them and that made him feel confident. He imagined his father's homecoming and the praise that he would receive. At the yard he frequently used the phrase, 'when Pa returns', and when his uncles exchanged glances he chose not to notice.

Mary-Ann didn't speak much but she showed that she was aware of the passage of time because, as December progressed, she would spend hours standing at the door looking for her husband. The fire would go out and the house would be cold but she did not notice. In the evening when the others came home from work and school they would find Tom and Elizabeth huddled together in the pen, their skin cold and blue; they did not cry until Caroline had given them some warm milk. 'Ma,' she would say, 'look at them. They will be ill.' Mary-Ann's head would swivel round towards them but then swivel back as if she'd seen nothing: she saw only the emptiness of the street, not even acknowledging her other children as they came home. Eliza and Mary wondered what their mother would do after Christmas if Pa was still absent.

Three days before Christmas there was a knock at the door. Mary-Ann stopped the chair from rocking and looked up. Henry opened the door and Hannah stood there with baby Martha in her arms. Mary-Ann looked at the floor and resumed her rocking.

'I've brought her home. She no longer takes from me. I thought you might want to have her here with it being Christmas.' Martha started to cry. Her mother ignored her so Eliza stepped forward and took her from Hannah.

'Yes,' agreed Henry, 'it will be good for her to be here when Pa arrives.' Mary-Ann gasped and stopped rocking again. She looked at him.

'Is he coming? Do you know?'

'He said he would, in his note.' Henry turned to Hannah. 'Is all the family coming to the yard on Christmas Eve as usual? We can celebrate his return then.' Mary-Ann's eyes brightened but Hannah's eyebrows were raised as her eyes met Henry's. He looked away and, ignoring the cavern that was developing in his stomach, continued, 'Is each family bringing food again?'

'They are,' she replied.

'We will contribute something.' Henry glanced at his sisters who, having noticed Hannah's reaction, nodded hesitantly.

'We'll meet up again then, Aunt Hannah.' He gave his mother a reassuring hug and she smiled up at him. She smiled! His heart expanded with joy and muffled the cavern's echoes.

As Hannah stood up to leave she glanced from Henry to Eliza and Mary.

'Don't worry too much about food. Everyone always brings more than we need,' she said as she left. Martha started to cry again. This time Mary-Ann took her from Eliza and hugged her.

On the day before Christmas Henry went along to the Angel Inn on Market Place where the coach from London stopped. Four o'clock came and so did the coach but his father was not on it. Disconsolately he turned for home.

'No matter,' said Mary-Ann when he arrived alone. 'He'll have come on the earlier coach and gone straight to the yard. I expect he's there now, waiting to surprise us.' At this Henry smiled but then he noticed the tears in Eliza's eyes. He looked at his mother and his smile froze. Reality was cruel and would hurt her.

They arrived at the yard, Henry and William carrying between them the huge pot of rabbit stew that was their contribution to the feast. When they opened the door to the yard they smelt the Christmas spices. Henry remembered past

Christmases when they would rush in to see how the yard had been decorated with cheery shouts of 'Merry Christmas' from his mother and father, which would be echoed by the rest of the family. Now the room fell silent as they walked in. Mary-Ann pushed past him.

'Where's he hiding then? Where is he?' She looked round the yard at groups of happy people who were staring at her. She looked at Henry and her eyes grew wide. 'You said that he would be here. You said.' Mary-Ann was not shouting: she was screeching. Mary and Hannah, her sisters-in-law, came to her and led her to a chair. Others came and took the rabbit stew for the table and the younger children ran to their cousins. Robert and James came to Henry and William and gave them drinks, patting their shoulders and telling them how well they were doing. Henry stood as if in a dream: it was Christmas and he was still the man of his father's household. For how much longer? The question persisted until after his third drink.

The New Year came and the bitterness of winter arrived. Mary-Ann had started to care for her family again, much to the relief of her older children, although she still sat silently staring at the fire and agitating her rocking chair all evening after the younger children had gone to bed.

'What do you think has happened to him?' Eliza asked one evening.

Henry shrugged. 'Who knows?'

Mary-Ann looked up. 'I know. He was caught out by the suddenness of the cold weather. He'll be still in London. He'll come back in the spring when the weather improves. You'll see.'

'But Ma the stagecoaches run all winter,' William pointed out.

'Yes, but I remember your father always said that only fools travel when the ground is hard with frost. And your father is no fool.' William looked unconvinced although Henry sat forward.

'Did he really say that?' he asked.

Mary-Ann nodded. 'This baby will come in March or April and perhaps he will be home by then.'

'What will we do when the baby comes? Will Aunt Hannah and Aunt Mary come and help again?' asked Eliza.

'I expect so. If your father's here he will fetch them. If not the babe will be a welcome home for him when –.'

'Ma,' interrupted William, 'what if he doesn't arrive? What if he's in the bottom of the Bure, robbed when he tried to find a passage on a boat? Or robbed by a carter who'll have offered to take him to London – for a deal less than the stagecoach would have cost him – and then dumped him in Waveney forest? He may not come home at all Ma!'

Mary-Ann sat with her mouth open for a few moments but then jumped up from her chair, rushed over to William and slapped his face.

'Do not say that. It is not true. He's coming home, he's coming home I tell you!' Mary-Ann flung herself into her chair and set it rocking furiously.

Henry stood still whilst the scene imprinted itself on his mind. It would stay there forever.

Days went by and turned into weeks. The only difference William had made was that his mother did not acknowledge him: if he spoke she did not hear and when she looked in his direction it was as if she did not see him. She spoke to her other children but she did not mention their father. She looked after her family and had resumed her habitual humming, especially when she was preparing for the coming baby. William became morose: sometimes he spoke with his older sisters but not to Henry who was infected with his mother's optimism.

One evening towards the end of February there was a knock at the door. Eliza answered it.

'Uncle James!' she exclaimed with pleasure, 'come in.'

'It's your Henry I'm looking for,' James replied.

'What is it?' Henry asked as he wiped the fish-oils from his chin and stood up. James held up his hand to stop him.

'No wait, finish your food.'

'That was the last mouthful. What do you want?' Henry frowned but James smiled.

'It's just something I thought you might like to do. You have so many responsibilities here.' He paused. 'I am a bell-ringer, as was my father before me. He hoped that someone from the next generation might take it up. Your cousin Robert – my brother's oldest – he tried but he just couldn't do it.' Henry grinned at the thought and James smiled back. 'Yes, we all know how clumsy he is. My James and Edmund are too young, as is your William,' looking up he saw William scowling, 'but what about you? Would you like to try?' Henry looked around the room hesitantly.

'Go on Henry,' said Mary. 'We can manage here without you for one evening a week.'

'I'm on my way now. Are you coming?' James asked but Henry already had his coat on and was standing by the door.'

'You can come next year if you like William, when you've grown some more,' suggested James but William just shrugged. James looked at Henry who nodded towards the door and the two men went out.

'What's wrong with William?' James asked as the two men walked up Garrison Walk towards Caister Road.

'Ma has said that she thinks Pa will come in the spring because he doesn't like to travel in the winter. William tried to make her more realistic and wants us all to do the same. I am happy that Ma is eating properly and able to look after the family again and I don't see the point of making her unhappy. That will come eventually if Pa does not return but I feel she should be left with the contentment she has for now.'

'And what do you think about your father?' The two men turned south into Caister Road and walked towards St Nicholas's church.

'Ma may be right. After all she knows him better than we do. But no, I fear that if he was coming home he would have come by Christmas like he said.'

'And what do you feel about that?

'May I speak my mind? He is your brother and I would not offend.'

'Of course. I would not have asked you if I was not prepared to hear what you really thought.'

'I'm angry. Angry for Ma. It's as if she's been widowed. She was so looking forward to the cottage at the yard but now, even if he returns, Uncle Robert has moved in. We're still in Garrison Walk.'

'If he comes back a rich man you will move from there. I'm sure he only wants the best for your mother.'

'But she was more than content with the prospect of moving into the cottage at the yard. You should have seen her those few days between grandmother's funeral and when he left. She was like an excited child and couldn't stop singing. It's no exaggeration to say that he has been as mean to her as if he'd locked her in the privy for the last six months.'

'It may yet work out well.'

'Even if he comes back a rich man I don't think my mother will easily recover. And as for me, I don't want to be a rich man's son and go away to university or the law courts or some such thing. I'm a millwright and I enjoy it – and I have lost my future share in the yard.'

James laughed. 'Spoken like a true Spandler. Maybe if he comes back rich we'll let you buy your way back into the yard.' Delighted, Henry grinned at him. Then his smile faded.

'If he doesn't come I will only ever be an employee of the family, like the other men. I will never have any say in the decisions that are made – and young Robert will eventually become master-in-charge.' James met Henry's and for a moment he looked as if he was about to say something but then he shook his head as he led the way into the church.

After the bellringing finished Henry didn't go home. He decided to go and see Genevieve with whom, before his father had left, he had become acquainted. He had spoken to her many times as he mingled with the congregation after church. She stirred his affections; her face was sweet; she was slight of build and he desired her. When James had called him a man six months ago Henry had been flummoxed but since then he'd been head of his father's household. He knew he was valued for his skills as a millwright and he had realised that James was right. He was a man and Genevieve was a young woman: he decided it was time for courting. He walked up Fuller's Hill and down onto North Quay. This brought him alongside the River Bure. He turned south and walked along the curve at the bottom of the hill, through Hall Plain and past the town hall. He stood for a few moments under the double row of trees that lined the east bank of the River Yare. Ahead of him he could see South Quay, the ships' masts dancing to the tune of the river as it slopped against their hulls, quiet now after the business of the day. To his left were large houses owned by merchants who made their fortunes trading with the owners of such ships. One of these merchants was Mr Watson, Genevieve's father. Henry stood outside the house and took a deep breath. Would she receive him?

The door was answered by a servant.

'Mr Henry Spandler to see Miss Genevieve,' he explained. He was shown through the high-ceiling hallway into a small room.

'Please take a seat,' the servant suggested and he left. Tentatively Henry sat on one of the large chairs, marvelling at the carpet beneath his feet. After a few minutes the servant returned.

'Miss Genevieve and Madam Watson will receive you now.' Henry followed the servant down the hallway and into another room.

'Mr Henry Spandler,' he announced and stepped aside to allow Henry to enter. Having rehearsed this scene in his mind many times, he smiled at the older lady in the room then crossed to Genevieve, took her hand, went on one knee and kissed it: he'd read such scenes in books and thought this was the proper thing to do. On the way down he was aware of her cleavage in a way that made his cheeks burn. He looked up to see her smiling and, thinking he'd pleased her, he released the breath he was holding. However, as he stood to his feet he froze: she and her mother were clearly amused.

'And what can we do for you?' It was her mother who spoke. He turned to her.

'I-I-I came.' He took a deep breath. 'I am a man now and will be a master millwright before long. I've come to court Miss Genevieve.' He smiled at Genevieve but was perplexed at her merriment and felt foolish, like a small child telling his schoolmaster that he'd completed his assignment. He thought that he should not have come and in the next moment his thoughts were confirmed. The door opened and Mr Watson entered. He looked at Henry and then at his wife, the expression on his face showing that he required an explanation.

'Mr Spandler here has come to court Genevieve. He's informed us that he is soon to be a master millwright,' she told him. For a few moments Mr Watson did not speak. His daughter was very beautiful and Henry was not the first young man who fancied himself as a suitor.

'You are young to be a master already, young sir.' he observed.

'My uncles have decided that I do not have much more to learn and they expect me to finish my apprenticeship next year.'

'And how long have you been an apprentice?'

'Four and a half years at the moment.'

'So, it will not be the full seven years. Not a proper master then. You will not be presenting to the guild?'

'My uncles will not allow our family business to be constrained by the old ways. I know almost as much as they do now.'

'Your family business? The Spandler millwrights?' Henry nodded as Mr Watson continued, 'They are highly thought of in the town – high mill at Southtown, they built that I think?'

'That's right, my grandfather -.'

'Yes, I remember his funeral a few years ago. A grand affair. So, the business is in the hands of the next generation now. Your uncles you say. But what of your father?' Henry felt hot as the colour in his cheeks deepened. He put his finger between his collar and his neck and moved his head from side to side to ease his discomfort but couldn't form coherent words with which to reply. Mr Watson frowned and pursed his lips. 'I have heard talk of a Spandler going to London to make his fortune but not returning.' Henry's eyes widened. 'Judging by your face that was your father.' Mr Watson looked towards the door. 'You have no prospects and I wonder why you have come. I think you must leave.' He rang the bell and the servant appeared immediately, so quickly that Henry imagined he'd been listening just outside the door. As he went to leave he turned to Genevieve but she was looking at her mother. They were both tittering and he knew he was the object of their mirth. Trying to hide his dismay, Henry left the house.

As he retraced his steps the cold air was sharp against his burning cheeks. Unbidden, his mind replayed the experience. He stopped again under the trees and wished he could turn back the clock to when he'd paused there before.

However, he knew that even if he could, he would do the same again. Suddenly he comprehended how much his circumstances had changed since he first spoke with Genevieve more than six months ago. His father had not only left him with the responsibility of his family but in selling his share he had affected Henry's life beyond the walls of Spandler's millwrights' yard.

3

For the first few weeks after the birth of her baby Mary-Ann was happy. Members of the family came visiting and Hannah and Mary, the wives of Henry's uncles, accompanied her when she was churched. In the weeks after the christening, however, she started to cry.

'I don't think Ma's feeding him properly,' Eliza shared with Mary whilst they were cooking the following evening. Mary-Ann was rocking and if she heard she gave no indication. 'Caroline told me that when they arrived home yesterday he was asleep on her knee with her breasts dangling above him slowly dripping milk. Ma and the baby were both cold. She said that as soon as she touched him he jolted awake. He looked distressed and his mouth was open as if he was crying yet he made no sound. She held him to the nipple and he fed hungrily. I wonder if Ma picked him up to feed him and then forgot what she was doing and just sat there.'

'She'd not prepared any food when we came in tonight. Just like she used to when Pa first left.' The girls looked at each other.

'She's become sad again. I think she's realised that he's not coming.'

'Is that what you think? He won't return?'

'I've decided that if he comes I'll be surprised. I'm living my life as if he was dead.' At this Mary-Ann started to keen, softly at first but getting louder. The girls went to her. Mary put her arms around her shoulders and Eliza knelt down beside her and looked into her face.

'Ma, Ma, please don't cry.'

'We're here Ma. Stop Ma, stop.'

It was as if she could neither see nor hear them. The younger children had gone quiet and stared at her. Then suddenly she was silent and the rocking resumed.

When Caroline came home from school three days later the baby was on the floor. He had fallen on his head and was dead.

'I don't think she knew that she'd dropped him,' Eliza explained to Henry, 'because when Caroline cried out and picked him up Ma looked puzzled and said she thought he was in his cradle.'

'Well the Constable is coming later. He knows us and knows what's happened. He'll ask her things but I don't think she'll know. He'll have to listen to what Caroline says.'

'Ma,' Eliza's lip quivered, 'will she be in trouble?'

'No, because he'll probably say that she's insane.'

'Ma, insane! That's unjust.'

'How else can you describe her?' Eliza frowned but Henry continued,' you know that if she's not insane she'll be accused of killing her baby?'

'It's just that, well, Ma – she's always looked after us so well. She would show us how to laugh when things were going wrong.'

'Yes she made everything right for us when we were younger. I feel sorry for Thomas, Elizabeth and Martha – and that poor baby. Pa's gone and it's as if they've no mother either.'

'Neither have we,' Eliza sighed, 'but I suppose we don't need her as much as they do.'

Summer arrived suddenly when the weather at the beginning of July became very hot. Consequently the school finished two weeks early because many of the children were absent in order to work in the farms near Caister and the nursery in Yarmouth.

'I think Grout's might take Caroline on to help with the extra fetching and carrying now that we've moved into the new building,' suggested Eliza, 'although I don't think she'll earn as much as sixpence for a full week's work.

'Yes, but if they keep her on through August and into September she should have enough for her schoolbooks in the autumn,' replied Henry. The small children were in bed but Caroline, Hannah and Rachel had been allowed to stay up because the discussion was about them.

'I could try and find work at the nursery,' suggested Hannah.

'They might not take you on,' said William, 'you're small.'

'Yes, but I'm strong,' replied Hannah, 'let me try.'

Henry nodded and then turned to nine-year-old Rachel. 'I don't want you to find work. We need the money,' he drew a deep breath and looked at Mary-Ann, 'but I think it would be good if you helped Ma with the little ones.' His mother neither acknowledged what he had said nor stopped rocking.

'Help Ma keep them safe,' said Mary, 'and if you've time you could help with the cooking as well. It's just so much better for us all if meals are not so late. Elizabeth didn't eat more than three mouthfuls of her dinner before she fell asleep tonight.'

'I think you've the hardest job,' said Eliza, hugging the young girl to her, 'but I'm sure you'll manage.' Rachel's mouth formed half a smile.

Henry had two out of every four Saturday afternoons off. The other two he spent helping one of his uncles supervise the younger apprentices as they cleared up the yard in readiness for the next week's work. Hence one Saturday afternoon a few weeks later he was sitting in the yard in Garrison Walk with a sharp bodkin and strong waxed linen thread mending his work boots. Rachel was with him and she was patching the elbows of an old work shirt. In the corner of the yard she had marked out an area with driftwood from the pile that they used for the fire, in which the young children were playing.

'That's a good idea,' Henry commented, 'but how do you get them to stay in that space – especially Sarah and Thomas who can run!'

Rachel laughed. 'It's simple. If they step outside I take them indoors and tie them to the table next to Ma. I've only had to do it once or twice because they'd much rather be out here playing together.'

'It's sad that your Ma is indoors though.'

'Yes, and at first I tried to persuade her to come out as well, but she says we might not hear Pa at the door when he comes back.' Henry frowned and concentrated on repairing the boot. After a while he looked up towards the fields that belonged to the nursery.

'Look I can see a group of them working – over there towards Apollo Walk. I wonder if Hannah's amongst them?'

'Last week she was near enough to wave. She said that they're hoeing today – and tomorrow.'

'Tomorrow? But it's Sunday.'

'She says things don't stop growing just because it's Sunday and they're paying her a whole penny for the day. As she only gets fourpence halfpenny for the other six days she's pleased to work it.'

It was three days later that the accident happened. At the end of each day the workers had to carry their hoes back to the nursery buildings. As they were walking along a young boy who, a few days earlier, had developed a fever, collapsed. Hannah was behind him and as he fell his hoe flipped backwards out of his hand and struck Hannah across the face. The wound streamed with blood and one of the workers gave her some old sacking which she held against the wound to staunch the bleeding. Unfortunately the sacking had previously contained partly-decomposed manure. Eliza cleaned the wound thoroughly when she got home but it was not enough. Septicaemia set in and within a week Hannah was dead.

Henry felt as if he was falling into a pit: the life his father had imposed upon him was out of his control.

It was the end of the working day a few days later and Henry reached for his jacket. His mood darkened as he thought of returning home but as he crossed the yard Robert beckoned to him.

'Henry, we need to discuss the best way of repairing the split in the main beam of Robertson's mill.' Robert looked from James to Henry as he spoke and James nodded. 'We're going for some ale. Are you coming?'

'We were thinking that you may have ideas we haven't thought of,' added James. 'Besides, it's warm and I'm thirsty!' Henry grinned: he enjoyed trying to work out solutions with his uncles and pushed thoughts of home away.

'If it's the main beam I should think we pull the whole thing down and start again – but let's take the diagrams with us,' Henry replied. Robert looked through a basket of rolled up documents on his desk.

'Here it is. Let's go.'

They entered the King's Arms and sat in one of the booths. Edmund was near the bar and scowled when he saw Henry with them. An hour later, after two tankards of ale and a lively discussion, Henry returned to Garrison Walk. As the weeks passed he started calling in at the King's Arms whether or not they were having a discussion: he found a tankard of ale took the edge off his despair as he returned home.

Months passed, summer waned and there was a chill in the air: after the fire was no longer in use for cooking, William put some extra wood on it to build it up. As he refilled the wood basket, he made a mental note to himself to go down to the shore after the first of the winter storms and collect some more driftwood. There were so many wrecks along the Norfolk coast that many households were able to feed their fires with the wood from the wrecked ships but William knew that everyone's stocks would be low. He'd have to be quick.

4

'Shall I read?' asked Rachel as she reached for the book from the shelf by the fire. She knew the answer. She opened 'Tales of the Crusaders' by Sir Walter Scott and, when she looked up, all her sisters and brothers were smiling. Mary-Ann did not smile but she did stop rocking.

Suddenly the door opened.

A man stood on the step.

'What do you think you're doing,' snarled William. The man stepped forward, holding out his arms.

'W-Will,' he quavered.

Everyone looked at him. Caroline wrinkled her nose.

Henry stared. 'Pa? Is it you?' The man fixed his gaze on the floor, nodded imperceptibly, and shuffled into the middle of the room. Mary-Ann looked up at him, shook her head and resumed rocking her chair. Eliza stood and reached for the water bucket. She poured its contents into a large, battered pan that they used to heat water to do the washing. She put the pan on the fire as William took the empty bucket from her.

'I'll go to the pump. It'll take a lot of water to clean him.'

Henry watched his father beginning to scratch as he warmed up. 'I think we'll need to strip and wash him outside, cold though it is,' he suggested. 'I'll pull the tub as near to the back door as I can to shield him from the wind.'

Eliza realised straight away why her brother was suggesting that their father, thin and ill though he looked, would need to be stripped and washed outside in the cold. 'There's boric acid on the shelves,' she said glancing up to the jar on the shelves above the fire. 'I remember Ma using it on Hannah when she came home from school with fleas. Soap him down thoroughly first. Then dissolve a good handful in the water and sit him in the tub. Lather his head whilst he's in the tub.'

Mary looked in the mending basket which was full of clothes. 'There's a pair of your old trousers in here Henry. Bit worn round the bottom and I was going to cut them down for William. Actually, I meant to do it last night but Martha was fretful and there wasn't time. It's just as well.' The man went to sit down in the chair that had been his but which, since Christmas, Henry had been using.

'No, don't sit there until you're clean,' said Eliza. 'Sit on the bench where there is no cushion.' Caroline, Hannah and Rachel bumped into each other in their haste to move off the bench. The man sat down but did not speak. Minutes passed.

'This water is becoming hot now.' Mary looked at her mother and her sisters. 'I'll put a towel to warm and then I think we'll go upstairs and leave him with Henry and William while he cleans himself up. Come on Ma.' Mary-Ann looked to be about to argue but then she stood up. The girls picked up the younger ones and they all went upstairs leaving Henry with his father. When William came in with the extra water Henry was giving him a chunk of bread smeared with cold bacon grease

'Come on now Pa,' said Henry gently as he finished chewing, 'let's remove these clothes.' They went outside into the cold where Henry and William helped their father undress. They glanced at each other as they realised how thin his limbs were. Two of them were misshapen.

Twenty minutes later they were back indoors. Henry Spandler, dressed in his eldest son's old clothes, was still shivering. William turned towards the shelves above the fire to reach the canister of tea. At that moment there was a knock at the door, making their Pa jump and look afraid. Henry noticed his reaction, frowned and moved to the door. He opened it and his father's brothers Robert and James walked in.

'You're home.' Robert said before turning to James. 'Edmund was right. He said he thought he'd seen him.' Henry grimaced as he imagined how his father would have been described by Edmund.

'Sit in your chair, Pa,' said William gently. William handed him a beaker of tea and he cupped his hands round it and slurped. Henry smiled as he watched his father relax. No-one spoke for a few minutes during which time this man, who had changed so much that he looked like a stranger, gazed at each of his brothers in turn. Then he started to speak.

'When I reached London I set up a workshop. By the end of September last year I was employing three men. We made metal joints, kitchen gadgets, trinkets for the ladies, in fact anything. Word spread that we were inventive and could make the things people needed. By the end of October the business had doubled in value. I sold it and the buyer, a man called Jack, offered me a very high price for it – far more than it was worth. I was fooled. He insisted on paying me with gold and I was robbed before I could get to the bank. They broke my arm and my leg. I was taken to the poor hospital where I eventually recovered although my body fevered and by the time I had regained my wits there was no trace of the robbers, or the man who had bought the business. He had sold it again and disappeared. Not that I could prove anything anyway. I walked most of the way home although some carters, seeing my limp, took pity on me and carried me without charge.'

'You're here now.' Robert put an arm on his shoulder.

'You'll soon regain your strength,' said James.

'Yes, but I'll never climb out onto a mill-cap again,' he stated.

'Pa, rest for now and eat as well as we can afford. When the fine weather comes in the spring it may help. You do not need to worry about work for now.' As he spoke Henry smiled at his father who had managed to meet his eyes for the first time since he came home. He did not look well and he had been hurt while he was away but now he was home. Henry suddenly felt weary with the responsibilities that had been his for the past fourteen months and he sighed. His father was home!

'That's not yer Pa,' said a voice from the stairs. Mary-Ann had come down behind Eliza and Mary and was standing on the bottom step.

'Ma, it is,' corrected Eliza.

'My Henry is broad and strong and walks straight.' asserted Mary-Ann. 'This man is a weak and frail cripple. It can't be him.'

'Pa will get stronger Ma, now that he's home with us,' said William.

'Pa,' said Eliza, 'Hannah died last month.'

Henry's mouth opened. 'Hannah? My Hannah? How?'

'An accident. She was working at the nursery,' explained Mary. 'The younger children are all well. Ma was with child when you left and he was born in March but died shortly after.' Her father shrugged as Mary pointed to her mother. 'Ma has been very troubled whilst you have been away.' Mary-Ann sat down suddenly in her chair and commenced her rocking. 'This is how she's been most of the time.' The man's eyes filled with tears. He reached out towards her but she did not look at him or stop rocking.

'Mary-Annie,' he said, using his pet name for her. 'I'm sorry. I should not have gone.'

'Bit late for being sorry Pa,' snapped William, his lips tight and his nostrils flared.

'I wanted to have enough money for you,' he continued, ignoring his son. 'I wanted you to have a proper house with beautiful furniture and servants. Mary-Annie, I wanted you to be happy.'

'Yes, I see it's you now, Henny,' she replied, matching his pet name with one of her own, 'but you can see that I am not happy. The cottage at the yard would've been grand enough for me. Now this is what we have. This is where we live and where we'll die.' She looked away from him. There was no sound except for the rhythmic creaking of her chair.

5

Time did not stand still and, when Henry looked at his parents, he felt as if it was accelerating. He was bewildered. He'd never before considered his parents to be old but suddenly they were. They spent all day by the fire, Mary-Ann rocking as usual. His father, Henry, kept his chair as close as possible to hers and sat with his hand on her arm. He did not appear to be regaining his strength, as his Uncle James had suggested, but rather it seemed as if a sort of delayed shock had set in and he was being overtaken by the mental instability of his wife. Mary-Ann had not recommenced cooking and cleaning and Thomas, Elizabeth and Martha were not mothered. Sometimes, when Eliza and Mary returned from work, they would recall when life was normal: then they would come in to find their mother, the evening meal prepared, sitting on the bed surrounded by little children while she told them a story or they sang songs together. Henry's relief on the evening of his father's reappearance had turned to despair. His position had not improved. Yes, his father had returned, but all that meant was that he now had the care of both his parents and they were becoming senile.

Caroline and Rachel had felt sad at the end of the summer when they'd first returned to school with Sarah after Hannah's death. Now, at the end of the week following their father's homecoming, they came home carrying Sarah between them. She had developed a fever during the day. The following day when they came in from school Sarah was curled up next to her mother's chair; her eyes were watering; her nose was running and she was shivering.

'Ma, why do you not take Sarah onto your knee,' Caroline remonstrated, 'and cover her with a blanket and cuddle her like you used to do for me was I was small?'

'I have your Pa,' replied Mary-Ann as she stroked Henry's arm.

'But Sarah is poorly, Ma, she needs you. What about the little ones? Have they had anything to eat today?'

'No but neither has your Pa. I can only sit and comfort him. He is a broken man.' Caroline and Rachel exchanged glances as Rachel started to prepare vegetables.

'There was only one large piece of wood in the fire basket,' their father muttered to Caroline's back as she bent over the fire to blow the barely glowing embers.

'There's plenty more in the yard by the privy where it's always been,' replied Caroline without turning around, as the kindling flamed and she added some small sticks.

'Your Pa cannot do it. He is a broken man,' repeated Mary-Ann. Caroline did not reply but dashed through the back door with the basket to fetch more wood before the sticks burnt up.

Rachel gave Thomas, Elizabeth and Martha a piece of raw carrot each and some warm milk and, as the warmth of the fire reached them, they played. Rachel lifted Sarah from the floor and sat her on her parent's bed. She held a cup of warm milk to her lips and Sarah quickly took two large gulps and then coughed and shivered, flopping against Rachel. She laid her down and covered her with a blanket.

'That's our bed. Don't lie her there. We need it. It's ours.' Mary-Ann pouted at her daughter. Rachel did not reply but again exchanged glances with Caroline.

'I do not need to stay at school,' said Caroline later that evening, 'I will be fourteen at Christmas and I am not learning anything new. Let me stay at home and care for Ma and Pa and the younger ones.' She went on to explain to Henry how she'd found Sarah when she came in. Henry closed his eyes and rubbed his forehead.

'What do you think Pa?' he asked, looking at his parents who were observing them from their chairs by the fire.

His father shrugged. 'Do what you like Henry. It's your decision.'

'But Pa...'

His father shook his head. 'It shouldn't be like this, I know, but I can't be the head of this house any more. It's up to you.' Henry ground his teeth to keep himself from crying out.

'I'm a girl and I do not need more education,' said Caroline quickly, noticing her brother's consternation. 'One day I may wed and being here will prepare me for that better than school.' Henry nodded while he stared in perplexity at his father.

At the yard the following morning Henry had just finished supervising William and Edmund as they attempted to chisel a disc of wood to turn it into a cog-wheel. Each of the individual cogs had to be cut accurately in order for the wheel to work. These were apprentice pieces and would never be used in a mill but both of them were finding the task difficult. Henry told them they could take a fifteen-minute break while he went to the office to find his uncle, carrying the two cog wheels with him. When he arrived both Robert and James were in the office.

'How did they get on with that?' Robert asked.

'Hard. Edmund is slow and William is impatient,' he replied as he held out the wheels.

'That one has several chips in the cogs where the chisel has slipped,' observed James.

'Edmund became clumsier as he worked. Kept complaining he was tired. That's one reason why I've let them take a break.'

'He's always complaining he's tired,' said Robert, Edmund's father. 'It's usually when he doesn't want to do something.' They all laughed.

'And was there another reason for the break?' James asked.

'How's things at home?' asked Robert.

'That was the other reason. Pa's not improving. Last night he told me he could not be the man in the house anymore.' Robert and James exchanged glances. 'Ma's no better either. Caroline's leaving school to look after them and the younger children. Ma and Pa just sit in their chairs all day.'

Later that evening Robert and James came to Garrison Walk to visit their brother. They found him as Henry had described him. He sat passively stroking Mary-Ann's hand whilst Robert and James described the projects that were under way at the yard.

'Why not come back to work,' suggested James. 'We could find tasks for you at the yard. You would not need to go out to the mills.'

'What, you mean sweep up after the apprentices whilst they use the lathes and chisels? "Poor old lame Henry. Was a millwright once you know." That's how the men will talk as they laugh! No, I'm home now. I have my Mary-Ann. I hurt her when I went away and I need to stay with her now.'

'Henry, I wouldn't humiliate you like that!' Robert declared. 'I need help with the book-keeping. You could work in the office. There's always a good fire in there.' Henry hesitated as if he was about to agree until Mary-Ann picked up the pace of her rocking.

'No, I don't want to go to the yard.' His lips quivered and his voice shook. 'It reminds me of what I've lost and Mary-Ann needs me here.'

'Your family need you,' countered James, 'and they need their mother.' James turned to Mary-Ann but the only indication that she was aware of the conversation was that the rocking accelerated still further. It was becoming frenzied. 'They need you both to be father and mother to them.'

'Our Henry's done right enough while I've been away and I just want to stay here by my fireside.' Henry crossed his arms and stared at his brothers defiantly.

'But Pa,' interrupted William, 'you are our father, not Henry. We need you to earn some money. Hannah died because she was earning money that you should have earned.'

His father startled as if William had hit him; his lower lip pouted and he shook his head.

'I went to make more money than you could ever earn. It's not my fault that my Hannah died. It's your fault.' He turned to his eldest son. 'You should not have sent her out to work. Your uncles would have given you extra hours, if you'd asked, you idle boy.'

'Henry – your Henry, and William, have done as much work as I could give them. You cannot call them idle.' Robert's voice was uncharacteristically loud. 'I know you were hurt and that you're disappointed that your plans did not work but you cannot blame your sons for your daughter's death.' Robert looked at James.

'We did warn you not to go,' said James quietly. 'Now you need to face up to your responsibilities and come back to the yard. You will not find well-paid work elsewhere.' Mary-Ann stopped rocking and gripped Henry's arm tightly. He turned to her and put his other hand on top of hers.

'It's alright, I'm not going,' he said to her while his eldest son rolled his eyes to the ceiling. He turned to his brothers. 'You can see what she's like. I'm staying with her, and besides I don't need your charity. Good-day.' He pointed to the door and Robert and James, with a glance round the room, picked up their coats and left. The door closed leaving silence.

The following morning at the yard Robert and James called Henry into the office.

'After we left your house last night we went to see our sisters,' Robert began. 'You're a young man and a good son – and you have done enough. You need to make your own life. We've worked it out between us. Eliza can come to us where she can help with our younger children and she can bring your Thomas with her. Mary can go to your Aunt Elizabeth with Martha and young Elizabeth.'

'William will come to us,' said James, 'and our youngest sister Hannah will have Rachel and Caroline.'

Henry felt as if he had stopped breathing. His heart dropped as he thought he'd failed but at the same time he realised that this would mean his responsibilities would be lifted. His heart rose but then fell again.

'But what of Ma and Pa? And you did not mention Sarah.' He frowned.

Robert drew a deep breath. 'We've enquired at the workhouse. There is a doctor that calls there regularly. We would give a donation each year from the yard so they would be well looked after.'

The colour drained from Henry's face.

'The w-workhouse,' he faltered. 'I could not do that to them.'

'They are all unwell. They will be cared for. You can live your lives.' James stated the facts without emotion.

'I thank you for your concern but I don't think I can agree. I will ask the older ones tonight and if they want to we will do it. But I think they will be as uneasy with the idea as I am.' His uncles nodded.

'We are not surprised at your answer,' said Robert, 'but we would urge you to tell the others and then think about it for a few days before you decide. Don't answer too quickly.'

Henry told William as they walked home from the yard. William didn't reply and for a few minutes they walked in silence. Eventually he spoke.

'I wonder if it would not be for the best.' Henry's chest tightened at William's words. 'Ma and Pa are becoming more and more decrepit by the day. This way the younger ones would be well cared for and well, for us, our lives would become normal again.'

'But Ma and Pa – and little Sarah!' cried Henry. 'Why, she would be amongst strangers! How could my life ever be normal if I knew they were in that place and I had put them there? Besides Caroline would never agree to Sarah going there.'

'Well Caroline is as sentimental a fool as you are.' Henry did not reply and they walked on in silence until they reached the corner of Garrison Walk.

'I'll wait here for Eliza and Mary so I can tell them,' Henry said. 'You go on and talk to Caroline. Not where Ma and Pa can hear you, outside if you need to. We'll only tell them when we know what we're doing – that's if...' William turned abruptly and walked on leaving Henry staring after him.

'Why have you waited for us?' Mary asked. Henry told them and both the girls momentarily stopped walking, their eyes opened wide and their hands flew to their mouths.

'No,' said Eliza.

'They'd split them up in the workhouse. Sarah would be on her own with the other children. Pa and Ma would be separated.'

'I'd thought of Sarah not being with Ma and Pa but I didn't think of Ma and Pa not being together. No, we can't, it would kill her.'

As they walked down Garrison Walk they could see that William and Caroline were outside by the front door.

'Well I hope you three agree with us,' jabbered William as they approached. 'We think it's very good of our uncles and aunts to help us like this. They are our elders and if they have suggested it then we ought to agree with them.'

Henry, Eliza and Mary stopped in amazement. Caroline looked discomforted at their reaction.

'I-I'm a bit unsure really,' she stuttered. 'William said...'

'I don't know what William has told you.' Eliza's voice was sharp. 'We are not wanting to do this.'

'Did Uncle Robert really suggest it?' Caroline asked.

'Yes, I think he could see that we were all upset when they were here last night. The aunts and uncles are giving us a way out of our situation – but only if we want it. Uncle Robert said not to decide immediately but to think about it for a few days.'

'If William wants to go, let him,' suggested Mary but Henry was shaking his head.

'If he goes we would lose his wage, and we are only just managing with it.'

'Henry,' insisted William, 'think about it. You hate this.' He nodded his head towards the open door of the cottage. 'This is your chance to be free of it all.'

'I'll admit that for one moment when it was first suggested I was delighted. And it is not for Pa that I hesitate. He has brought this about. If he hadn't gone to London he would now be the master-in-charge of the yard and we would all be happily living there. No, it's Ma and little Sarah. I cannot do it to them.'

Henry and William stared at each other. No-one spoke.

'We'd best go in then,' said Eliza eventually. 'Wait a minute, what's that smell?' She stopped in amazement and turned to Caroline. 'Meat?'

Caroline nodded. 'Mr Greensome from the nursery called round today with two rabbits that he'd caught. Thought we might like them.'

'That'll make us feel better, with our bellies full of meat,' declared Henry.

'Yes, but it'll not make the problems go away though, will it?' William glared at them all. 'Use your heads. They'll be dead before long anyway.'

'In that case we can wait until after the funerals and carry on with our lives then.' Eliza glared at her younger brother before she led the way indoors.

6

Great Yarmouth, the town where they lived, was undergoing change. Inside the town most people inhabited narrow alleys, called Rows, down the middle of which ran open drains. These were built in an east-west direction and sloped down towards the river enabling the muck to be flushed out by wind and rain during the storms. As the town expanded the market had grown and an area to the east of the market place had become known as the Shambles: it was where the butchers established themselves. This was inevitably an area that produced a great deal of waste. At first this was taken across the market place and put into the open drains of the Rows. However this meant that the drains often became blocked. The heat of the summer caused outbreaks of disease in the town which was attributed to the smells from these drains which ran close to the houses in the Rows. Since then, for many years it had been placed in carts that were wheeled along Garrison Walk to the rubbish dumps. Now it had been decided that a new drain needed to be built. This started at the slaughter houses outside the walls, went behind the factory houses, through the churchyard and nursery gardens. Then it crossed Caister road and went down Garrison Walk to the river. They had started digging it at about the same time as Henry's father had returned from London and, although work had paused in the middle of winter when the ground froze, the drain was in use by Easter. The smell from the soil heaps that the family had hated was now eclipsed by the stench of the drain.

In spite of this Henry's step as walked to the yard had spring that matched the season. He had always enjoyed his work but now it was the best part of his life and as he walked he felt himself relax: for the next few hours his responsibilities were those of a young man at work and his home life retreated into the back of his mind. If he saw his cousins laughing and joking he would be aware how different their lives were from his but for now the only problems he had to solve were those of hanging a new cog wheel. He was going out to a mill with his uncles that morning and they had told him that they would be supervising but that it was his job to direct the apprentices and make the final adjustments so that it spun true: he knew that if he got it wrong it would cause damage to both the new wheel and the one with which it meshed, costing the yard time and money. He also knew that his uncles had been talking about the end of his apprenticeship and they would be scrutinising him.

At the yard they loaded up the cart with all that they needed for the job. The horse, which was partly owned by the King's Arms next door, was being used by them to deliver small barrels of ale to some of the lodging houses in the town, so they needed to use man-power to pull the cart. The mill they were going to repair was only a short distance away across the Denes and Henry went to take one of the arms. Robert shook his head, his eyes dancing in merriment.

'No Henry. You're doing this as a millwright. The apprentices pull the cart. You walk with us.' Henry's stride lengthened and he was alongside his uncles in a moment, a huge grin on his face.

'Your father should be with us,' said James. Henry's smile faded.

'Yes, and I asked him to come. He said he wasn't interested,' he replied. Robert and James exchanged glances.

'He has changed so much,' Robert stated with a shake of his head. 'When you began your apprenticeship, and it became obvious very quickly that you had an aptitude for the craft, he was so proud. The old Henry would not have missed this for anything.'

'Unfortunately, my father is just that – old, old before his time. Wants nothing more than to sit by his fireside, which he does all day. William and I helped him wash again the other evening and I think that his arms and legs are even more wasted than they were when he first returned. In my head I know that he's my father but in my heart he is a stranger. Ma I feel affection for but he is just there.' Henry shrugged and looked at his uncles but they did not condemn him.

'It is your mother who keeps him there, is it not?' James asked. 'I think of that time when we visited and I suggested he worked in the office. He might have agreed if your mother was not there.'

'But he made her like she is now. He destroyed her. I was always so proud of him, I wanted to be like him but now.' Henry stopped. His uncles did not reply but Robert's hand made contact with his shoulder: it steadied him.

They had travelled out of Yarmouth along North Road and now turned east and set off across the Denes. Suddenly there was a shout behind them. Robert, James and Henry turned around to see Edmund being sick.

'I told you not to go out last night. You returned having had too much ale and this is what happens,' shouted Robert. 'As soon as you've finished you can get straight back to work.' Edmund did not reply but instead collapsed onto the ground. His father was incensed. He marched back to him and pulled him to his feet. James and Henry followed him.

'He is very pale,' said James. Robert glared at his brother whilst Edmund made strange gasping noises.

'I think he really is ill,' added Henry. Edmund was sweating, seemed unable to support his own weight and was leaning on his father. Robert, in exasperation dropped him back to the ground.

'Stay there then. We have work to do. Return home to your mother and she can fuss over you.' Abruptly he turned to the other apprentices. 'Pick up the cart. We're wasting time.'

A few minutes after they arrived at the mill Henry had forgotten all about Edmund. He was busy organising the apprentices to set up a pulley with which to raise the cog wheel because he would need its weight supported in order to fit it properly. The shaft upon which the cog wheel was to be threaded had an irregularly octagonal cross-section that varied along its length and Henry had taken measurements some weeks earlier. At the yard he had cut a mortise in the centre of the new cog wheel large enough to enable it to be pushed onto the shaft. This shaft ran at right angles to the main shaft that turned with the rotation of the sails and the two cog wheels had to mesh exactly if the strong Norfolk winds weren't going to pull the mill apart. The pulley that the apprentices had set up was attached to the top of it and they took its weight on the ropes, enabling Henry to manipulate it. At first it wobbled because it was loose and he had to ascertain it was at the right point along the shaft so that, once fixed, the cogs would alternate with the cogs of the other wheel smoothly. He made sure it hung perpendicularly to the other cog wheel and tightened the fit with small wedges inserted from either side and at different points around the inside of the mortise, measuring the angle after each wedge to maintain it correctly. It took a long time but Henry was working accurately and was not going to be rushed, especially by the apprentices. William muttered something as his arms began to ache and his stomach growled its hunger but Henry did not notice. It was the time of year when the days were short and, when Henry stepped back and declared that it was finished, there was not much daylight left. He nodded to the apprentices who, with a collective sigh, allowed the ropes to go slack so that they could be detached from the wheel. Henry turned to his uncles.

'All that's left now is for us to tidy up and return to the yard,' declared Robert.

'But do you not want to check it?' Henry held out the setsquare. However both his uncles shook their heads.

'We've watched you work. I am sure it's accurate,' stated James. Robert nodded.

'I cannot think of anything more difficult we can ask you to do unless we receive an order for a new mill. And, as neither of us has ever built a mill from scratch, I think,' Robert paused and looked from his brother to his nephew. 'I think that we three millwrights would have to work together on that.' Both the older men clapped him on the shoulder so that he nearly toppled forward. He looked up to see William grinning at him.

'Now I suggest we'll take you for some ale to celebrate,' said Robert, 'I'm sure these young ones can clear up here and take everything back to the yard.'

On the way back into Yarmouth they passed the point where Edmund had been taken ill that morning.

'It looks as if Ed managed to walk himself home then,' said Henry.

'I've noticed that he often becomes breathless easily,' said Robert. 'I wonder if there is more to it than laziness.'

'He looked more sickly than ale causes,' suggested James, 'although you say he had more than he should last night?'

'You should have heard the noise he made coming in. He must have drunk a great deal.'

'Or perhaps there is something wrong with him and a little ale made him clumsy,' Henry suggested.

'I see. Yes, I suppose I should have the doctor in.' Robert sighed. 'His mother tends to fuss him and this will just make it a deal worse. She won't be able to leave him alone and she'll object when I ask him to do any task at all.'

Later that evening, as he walked home, Henry's heart was heavy. He'd decided that he would tell his father that he'd completed his apprenticeship. However, he was not sure why he'd made that decision. As a young child he'd always enjoyed telling his father about his accomplishments but now it seemed pointless: he no longer cared. As he walked along Caister Road towards Garrison Walk he could already smell the new drain. He clenched his fists with resentment towards his father. The smell reminded him that, if his father had not been so foolish, he would now be walking back to the cottage at the yard and the new drain would not concern him at all.

Sarah was ill again. Her fever six months ago had left her weak and, although she'd managed to return to school just after Christmas, she'd remained pale and lethargic. As Henry tied his boots before leaving for work he watched as Caroline comforted her through another bout of coughing. The deepness of his frown demonstrated his concern; nevertheless he picked up his jacket and left for the yard. As he walked he breathed deeply and thought about the work awaiting him, pushing his home worries as far away as possible. He smiled: he was no longer an apprentice.

At the yard he busied himself with the steam engine. He took pride in bringing it up to steam before everyone arrived so that when they were ready to start work the power was available. He'd just turned away when his uncle James came towards him.

'Bad news I'm sad to say Henry,' he said. Henry drew a deep breath, his responsibilities at home overwhelming him for a moment. He let out the breath opening his eyes wide and raising his eyebrows. 'It's the bells Henry,' explained James, 'the dean came by and told me that we cannot ring them anymore.'

'Why not?' Henry asked, disappointment altering his voice: since his uncle had introduced him to bell-ringing it had become a favourite activity.

'The bands on the tower have corroded and two of them have broken completely. The vibrations could cause the tower to collapse. We're finishing all the jobs that we have here and next week they want us to take the bells down.'

One morning during the week when Henry was fully taken up with the bells Sarah's cough worsened. The others had just left for work and school when she coughed and coughed until she vomited. Mary-Ann was holding her and Caroline was clearing up the mess when she started with another spasm. It lasted so long that she made a strange noise when she drew breath. Caroline frowned and chewed her lip.

'Call it the chincough they do,' said Mary-Ann.

'What should I do Ma?' asked Caroline.

'I don't know.' Mary-Ann shrugged her shoulders.

'She's your child Ma.' Sarah looked at her mother but Mary-Ann looked away. Sarah's mouth opened and she mewed but there were no tears.

While she pondered what to do about Sarah, fourteen-year-old Caroline stirred the pot on the fire in which was the family's dinner. The previous evening Eliza had brought in a large pile of fish heads and Caroline had sorted through them, throwing away those which were stale enough to make her retch. The others she'd washed and put in the pan. Now, although her thoughts were on Sarah, she noted that the flesh was coming away from the bones and the cartilage was beginning to soften: soon that too would fall away and all but the largest pieces would dissolve into the liquid. She picked up the colander and went out into the yard where she opened a wooden box in which were three enormous pots. She untied the cloth from one of them and took from it a large handful of salted beans which she put into the colander. These were some of the glut of produce Hannah had been given at the nursery the previous summer. She rinsed them before adding them, together with some potatoes, to the fish broth. Later Caroline smiled as the family ate enthusiastically. William mashed one of his potatoes into the liquid.

'This broth makes the potatoes taste good,' he said, smiling at his younger sister. Caroline's smile became a grin. Just then Sarah started coughing. She put down her spoon and carried on coughing for what seemed to be a very long time. Everyone stared at her. When she finally drew breath her voice crowed.

'Ma called it the chincough but she said she didn't know what to do,' explained Caroline. They all turned to Mary-Ann but she ignored them.

'As it happens Susannah was talking about the chincough at the factory today,' Mary said.

'Did she know anything that would help?'

'Warm milk straight from the cow - she said that would soothe it. I could call in to one of the cowkeepers in town and see if I can buy some on my way home tomorrow.'

It seemed to be successful. A week later the cough had lessened in severity and two weeks after that Sarah was back at school. One time whilst she was ill she'd ventured to climb up onto Mary-Ann's knee and was not pushed away. After that she only had to smile at her mother to be invited up for a cuddle and even her father would allow her to snuggle between them. The older children noticed and were hopeful that this was the beginning of normality. However, it was limited to cuddling Sarah: the other children, including baby Martha, still went uncherished.

In the week before school finished for the summer break Sarah returned home fatigued, climbed onto Mary-Ann's knee and fell asleep. When they tried to rouse her for dinner she was uncharacteristically cross. The same thing happened on the following two evenings and by the weekend she'd started coughing again. However it did not seem to be as severe as last time and after a few weeks it stopped.

Eliza suggested, one Sunday at the beginning of July, that they all went for a picnic on the beach. Everyone assumed that Henry and Mary-Ann would stay behind but Sarah held out her hands to them and they stood up and followed her out of the cottage. Young Henry was amazed and the whole family was delighted: it was the first time since Pa's homecoming that they had all gone out together.

Sarah continued to cough sometimes but, although she was pale, she did not seem to be ill and after a while no one noticed it any more. She was three years older than Elizabeth and had been good at pacifying her when she was upset but suddenly she did not seem to have the patience any more. Caroline noticed: it was as if Sarah's personality was changing. Sometimes Caroline asked her if she was alright but she would just shrug her shoulders.

September came and Thomas started school. Sarah didn't go and, instead, climbed onto her mother's knee. She had been saying that her head hurt and twice in the past week she had held her head in her hands and wailed. On those occasions no-one could comfort her, not even Ma, and she would sit in the corner of the room and bang her head against the wall.

At the beginning of October her neck became stiff and she turned her back away from the light of the window, crying out if anyone came near her with a candle. Then she started to have fits: the tuberculosis, which had been present in the warm, fresh milk she had consumed to soothe her cough, had now reached her brain. Three days later she was dead.

7

A few days after the funeral Henry went to see his uncles.

'I think it is the new drain,' he said, 'I know it runs along the far side of the road from our cottage but it stinks worse than the rubbish heaps. It's only since it was dug that Sarah started with the coughing – she's dead and now Elizabeth's ill. It seems to affect the young ones more and I am worried about Martha and Thomas, although they're both well at the moment.'

'And what do you want us to do?' Robert barked. Henry jumped at the fierceness of Robert's question.

'I was hoping that perhaps they could come and stay with one of you, to remove them from the smell. I'm sure that's what made Sarah ill.' The two brothers looked at each other.

'What of our own children. They may bring some of the foul air from where you live and breathe it over them and make them ill also,' said James gently. 'My Hannah would not want them near George.'

'There is our sister Hannah who has no children.' Robert had sensed the young man's distress and spoke more calmly. 'I will ask her and see what she says. She may want one of the older girls to come as well and help.'

'Caroline is looking after Elizabeth and I need Eliza and Mary's wages to keep the house going. Rachel's eleven and she is good with the little ones. However she is at school still and I would like her to continue.'

'I will see what Hannah says. That may not be possible if you want them to be cared for.' Henry nodded.

'Henry, I wanted to ask you something,' said James, 'nothing to do with your family – it's about things here at the yard.' Henry smiled and the tension between them eased: whatever the question was it would be more easily solved than the ones at home. He looked expectantly at his uncle and James continued, 'I know you have been instructing the apprentices about the steam engine whenever the opportunity arises but I think you need, now that you've finished your apprenticeship, to have responsibility for one of them.' Henry frowned. Young Robert was so inept that it would be a challenge to train him; William was his brother and didn't always give him his full attention and he just did not like Edmund. James had seen his frown and smiled. 'It's none of those out there.' Henry's eyebrows rose. 'It's my eldest boy, Jim. He's learnt enough at school and I would like him to start his training here.'

Henry's smile became a grin and after a few moments he found his voice. 'I'd be delighted,' he replied. 'It's an honour that you trust him to me.'

Later that evening Aunt Hannah, their father's sister, came to the cottage at Garrison Walk. She was happy for Rachel, Thomas and Martha to come and live with her. She also agreed to Rachel staying at school because Thomas would be at school himself all day and she felt she could cope with little Martha by herself. The older children had known about Henry's visit to his uncles and its purpose. However, the younger children had no warning. Thomas was two years older than Elizabeth and Martha was two years younger: they were both shocked and clung onto Rachel when they realised she was coming with them. Elizabeth wailed in distress and climbed up onto her mother's knee.

'Don't cry,' Mary-Ann said when the front door closed, 'they'll come back soon.'

'No they won't Ma,' Eliza looked at Henry, William and Mary and then back to her parents huddled by the fire with Elizabeth between them. 'At least not until Tom and Martha are a great deal older.'

'But what have they done to deserve that? And what have I done to be separated from my children?' Mary-Ann's voice became high-pitched and thin as her chin wobbled.

Their father, roused by Mary-Ann's emotions, turned on his eldest son.

'What gives you the right to send them away? They're our children.' Henry was stunned. Before Henry had gone to see Robert and James they had discussed it next to their father in the room where he spent all his time and he had said nothing.

'You have shown no interest in them, or any of us, since you returned.' It was William speaking. He had stood up and was glaring down at his father.

'Show me some respect,' his father demanded.

'Pah! Respect? Why should I respect you? I heard you say to Henry that he had to make the decisions here. You lost my respect when you abandoned us and went to London.'

'I went to make us rich. We'd have had one of those large houses by the river.' His father's voice faltered. 'I-I had plans.' His head dropped.

No one spoke for a few moments. Henry looked at his father until he lifted his head. Then he stared into his eyes and started to speak in low, even tones.

'Without those plans we would have been living at the yard now – Sarah and Hannah would still be alive – and that other baby probably. No-one would have needed to go away. As it is we are here, breathing in the foulness of the town, whilst Elizabeth struggles for breath. That is why they have gone away. You demand that we show you respect – well I find that as impossible as William does. Yes, I respected you once. Now I despise you.'

'B-But I am your father. I care for you. I only wanted the best for you. Can you not forgive me my misfortune?'

Henry did not reply; he turned from his father and sat down on the bench. Out of the corner of his eye he could see Caroline being comforted by Eliza. His father jerked his head from one to the other of them. His eyes, wide and tear-filled, rested on his eldest son. Henry sensed his stare but ignored it.

He put his head in his hands. The family's misery was crushing him.

Suddenly he stood. Stopping only to pick up his coat, he left the house. He walked without consciously deciding where to go. His steps, long and fast, powered with adrenaline, took him to the seashore. He went to the water's edge and, with exploding energy, skimmed stones into the water. Again and again the stones flew from his hand; again and again he picked a fresh one from the sand, uncaring whether any were shaped for bouncing well until, eventually, he stopped. His breath came quickly. He remembered laughing here, with his father, when he taught him to skim stones. Now his life was hateful. The last stone dropped from his fingers and he stood still looking at the horizon without focus until a large wave, borne on the incoming tide, swamped his feet, causing him to take a sudden deep breath. He turned and made his way from the sand. The sun had left the sky and he shivered. As he passed a tavern the warmth enticed him in. When he left hours later his step was unsteady but he was no longer distressed.

8

Six months passed.

Henry, and Jim his apprentice, were at a mill for the regular post-winter maintenance that was part of the contract they had with the mill owner. They had started by spraying the floor with water and now were side by side sweeping.

'Henry, why do we need the water?' Jim asked.

'It makes the task less unpleasant because it stops it all swirling into the air as we sweep,' replied Henry, pointing towards the dust and other debris in their sweeping piles. 'It's very important at a flour mill because the mixture of flour and sawdust can explode – although I have never heard of a water pump like this one exploding.'

Whilst Jim removed the rubbish Henry went outside to look at the water wheel: the buckets on it were cast iron. Henry picked up the new ones which they had brought with them. Jim had watched the casting of these at the yard. Henry knew that soon he would lose his apprentice for a few months while Robert gave him an introduction to iron-moulding. He smiled to himself when he remembered his own first attempt: he had been given a small lump of wood and was asked to chisel it into the shape of a three-inch bolt. After the casting the bolt which finally emerged from the sand mould had leant at an angle to its head and everyone had laughed. Uncle Robert had clapped him on the shoulder and roared that he wasn't an iron moulder and they would have to work out another way that he would be useful to the yard. That was before they had purchased Bessie, the stationary steam engine, which was now Henry's speciality. He turned back into the mill.

'Time for you to go paddling,' he said to Jim, nodding towards the channel down which the water flowed to the wheel. His voice betrayed his amusement: he remembered when he was the one standing in the race whilst water seeped into his shoes.

'How many new buckets have we got?' asked Jim.

'Seven – but we shouldn't need all of them. I think we replaced quite a few last year.' Jim removed four, which were corroded, and fitted new ones.

'The main drive rope is worn and needs replacing,' said Henry when he had finished, 'but I think we'll stop and eat first. Have you done any splicing?'

'A few years ago, Pa showed me, but I don't think my fingers were strong enough. I can remember being a bit cross because I could see what I needed to do but I couldn't do it.'

'So, do you think you could do it now?' Jim looked hesitant and Henry chuckled. 'I'll let you have a try and if you can't I'll show you again.'

The two young men sat down on a bench outside the mill overlooking a large expanse of water which was the reason for the mill's existence: the water-wheel raised water from the broad and emptied into a drainage channel which irrigated the fields. There were many such mills surrounding Yarmouth and Spandler's had contracts to maintain most of them.

Henry was often struck by the contrast between his two worlds.

At home his father continued to antagonise him even though Robert and James had visited to try and reason with him: they were told not to return. Being aware of his father's instability of mind Henry tried to block out his words but it was difficult. William said he ought to put his father in his place as he had abdicated his position as head of the house and sometimes he was inclined to do as William suggested but his upbringing constrained him. In contrast he enjoyed every moment of his working day, more so since he'd started teaching Jim: slaking Jim's curiosity gave him great pleasure especially when it was something complicated and he could see in his face when he understood. Henry sensed the admiration the youngster had for him and it went some way to restoring his self-esteem.

By the time summer returned Elizabeth had become very weak. She no longer slept upstairs with the other children but stayed with Mary-Ann and Henry in their bed near the fire. In the mornings, when Mary-Ann and Henry moved to their chairs, one of the older children would lift Elizabeth and take her over to them because her legs were now so thin that they could not support her weight.

One evening Elizabeth was curled up between her parents as usual. Her eyelids were closed and she was still. Eliza was watching her.

'Her skin is blue, almost transparent,' she said.

Mary looked up from the sock she was darning. 'At least she'd not coughing. She looks peaceful like that.' She smiled at her mother who smiled back and her smile made Henry smile: he liked to see her happy even if it was only briefly. After a few minutes Mary continued, 'Ma I don't understand. Why do you cradle Bets now? When Sarah was ill you would not allow Bets to climb onto your knee, only Sarah. Why do you wait until they're ill to love them?'

Mary-Ann shrugged. 'I cough, and Henry coughs. I do not want to breathe foul air on them while they are well. Bets,' she looked down and stroked her hair, 'Bets I cannot harm or help, I can only comfort. Like Sarah she will soon be dead.' Elizabeth's eyes snapped open and then immediately closed. The room was quiet and no-one was smiling any more. William stood up.

'I'm going out,' he said. Henry reached for his coat.

'Do you mind if I come with you?' William shook his head. The two young brothers walked up the street without speaking. At the corner they turned along North Road into the town. William broke the silence.

'You must not blame yourself.'

'In my head I know that, but my heart is sad. I wonder if we should have put them in the workhouse when the uncles suggested it. I have regrets.'

'Don't. I know I disagreed with you at the time but all we discussed it and the decision was made to keep them here. You suddenly had to become the man in charge of us and I think you have done well. It's Pa who ought to have regrets.'

'Yes,' agreed Henry, 'and I meant what I said to him last year. I despise him although it ought to be said that he was unfortunate. I'm sure he didn't deliberately lose the money.'

'Or he did and made up the story about his business and being robbed,' suggested William.

'No, I despise him for taking the risk – but I think he was almost successful. I believe that he was on his way home with more money than he left with. I am just angry that he has made everyone so unhappy, especially Ma.' They had drawn level with the King's Arms and Henry went to turn inside.

'I'm not coming in. I want just to walk,' stated William, 'and the sun is still in the sky. It'll be warm and stuffy in there, just like at home.' Henry hesitated, his hand on the door, but then turned.

'Come on then. Let's step out. All along the front to the column.' They grinned at each other, young boys again, and strode out in step with each other, past the railings of St Nicholas's church, across Church Plain and down St Nicholas Road. In less than five minutes they were walking south along the sands dunes. They passed Holkham Tavern outside which were several old men with tankards of ale.

'Let's walk to the column and then come back and sit and share a tankard here. The old fishermen are always good for a tale,' suggested William. Henry nodded. In another ten minutes they reached the column and looked up whilst their breath slowed.

'I've always wondered why it's Britannia on the top and not Nelson himself,' said William, 'and she's not even looking at the sea.'

Henry laughed. 'Yes, they say she's looking at Thorpe to see where her favourite son was born. She's important to sailors and so I suppose she was important to him.'

'There's a plaque here - but it's all in Latin,' said William.

'I can remember being told about it at school but I can't tell you what it says. I'm ready for that ale now, let's go back to the tavern.'

Later, their heads full of tales of the sea and their bellies full of ale, they returned to Garrison Walk. As they entered the house their parents looked up at them. Henry felt as though his father's eyes were boring into him as he crossed the room. He turned to look at him and their eyes locked on each other. Henry shook his head and his father's eyes filled with tears. Henry walked out of the door in the back of the house and went to the privy where he thumped the wall. Why did his father make him feel that it was he that was in the wrong?

9

It was two days later when the two brothers went out together again. This time, as they passed the entrance to Spandler's yard, they turned in at the King's Arms. The barman recognised them. Knowing their money would be forthcoming he filled a jug with ale from a barrel behind him. From the shelf above the barrel he lifted down a brass measuring container and used it to decant pints into two tankards. It was a process that was well practised and so was complete by the time they had crossed the room. Their cousins Robert and Edmund were at the bar.

'We don't see you in here very often these days, Henry,' said Robert as he raised his tankard.

Henry raised his own in reply but did not speak. His eyes flicked between his cousins, coming to rest on Edmund. Edmund looked into his eyes and it was Henry who looked away first. Edmund smiled and glanced round for admiration but no-one seemed to have noticed.

'My brother's no longer an apprentice of course,' said William to the young Robert, 'and I can see the other millwrights over there.' He nodded to one of the booths where their uncles, Robert and James, were sitting. Henry looked at him sharply but William's eyes betrayed his mischief and Henry laughed.

'You cannot see me off that easily,' he countered with a grin.

'Is it still difficult at home?' Robert enquired.

Henry nodded. 'However, I'd rather talk about something else. I know, how's the drawing? Are you doing anything different or is it still boats?

Robert's eyes lit up. 'I have thirty sketches in my collection now.'

Henry smiled. 'I remember when you showed them to me. You only had six then.'

'That was four years ago.'

Edmund, who had been looking at a group of men at the other side of the room, turned back to the conversation.

'We're not talking about your scribbles again, are we? Can you never talk about anything else brother?' At his words Robert cringed.

'I don't know why you call the drawings scribbles, Ed,' said William. 'I've seen them and they're very good. Or is that why you don't like them? You have no talent of your own and resent your brother's.'

Edmund stood to his feet; his lips were pushed together and his eyes were narrow.

'I'm going over there where I can have a proper conversation,' he said. He picked up his drink and walked away.

'I think you hit the nail on the head there, William,' chuckled Henry. His voice was raised and Edmund stopped momentarily but then continued without turning around. Robert's eyes showed his delight as William patted him on the back.

'I draw boats because I find them very interesting. To tell you the truth, I prefer them to the millwrights' yard.' Robert spoke quietly watching Henry for a reaction. 'Next week I'm going as a deckhand on a boat to Grimsby. We should be back the following week depending on the weather.'

'Your father knows this?' William asked.

Robert nodded. 'Yes, but Ed doesn't – and I'd rather keep it that way.' Henry and William nodded in understanding. 'My father is not too happy but I think he recognises that his eldest son has no aptitude for the craft – unlike you whose abilities are just what he would want mine to be.'

Henry's thoughts switched to his own father's indifference. He picked up his tankard and stared into his ale for a few moments before taking a large swig and shaking his head.

'So, you would be a mariner then?'

Robert's eyes lit up and he nodded. 'It's dangerous work, as the men on the boat I'm to sail with keep telling me – but I look at their captain and there's a good living to be made. He knows all the ports on this coast, from London up to the north of Scotland. Happen I'll change my mind after a few days at sea but for now I'm excited about making the trip.'

'We can see that!' Henry and William had never seen him so animated. Just then Edmund swaggered back across the room.

'Those men over there are looking for your father,' he informed them with delight. 'Something about owing them some money. I told them I knew of him.'

'And then led them over here,' hissed Henry as the men moved towards him, 'You fool!' Edmund laughed.

'Is this 'im?'

'Looks like 'im. Not so old.'

'It's his son,' Edmund told them.

'Is it indeed!' The biggest of the three men came up very close to Henry. 'Your father is in our debt.'

'Who says?' demanded William. Another of the men turned on him and took hold of the collar of his jacket and pushed him against the wall.

'What'ya doing,' called the barman, 'them's two respectable working men.' At the same time Henry was aware of Robert and James leaving the booth. They came and stood with them and the man let go of William. When Robert spoke his voice was measured and quiet.

'I'm sure there's no need for violence. Tell us what you know and why you think my brother owes you money.' Robert's assured authority stopped the men who appeared to sag slightly.

'Just need our money and that other young man – well we told him how we'd been treated and he told us that you were a merciless family. Said we'd have to force it from you.' They all looked around but Edmund had disappeared. 'Here,' the man fished in his pocket, 'we have owing chits we were given after he left.' Across the top was printed "Spandler's Engineering" and underneath "No Job Too Small". They all had different amounts of money on them and were signed "H. Spandler".

'That's not my father's hand,' declared Henry.

'It is not,' agreed Robert. He turned to the men. 'You say you were given these after he left?'

The third man, small and thin, coughed and stepped forward.

'Yes. Jack gave 'em to us. He said that he had been put in charge and Mr Spandler had gone back home to raise some more money and when he came back we would be paid. Weeks went by, by which time we all owed the lenders. Then suddenly Jack said the business was closing. All the equipment was sold but he said that the money was for the rent. We received nothing. Now our families are in the workhouse. We took to the road and set out to find him. It was hard, because we didn't know where he was from, so it's taken us a long time. Now – where is he?'

'My father is at home. He's a cripple and he can't help you.' The small man frowned at this but the one that had held William's collar now tried to throw a punch at him. He was caught by Robert and James and the barman shouted for them to throw him out.

'We're going,' called out the big man and he moved off across the room. Robert and James released the man they were holding and he shook himself and followed. The small man hesitated. The door closed behind the others and then he left.

'Well so much for coming out and leaving the worries of Pa at home,' muttered William. Henry grinned ruefully and they both looked at their uncles.

'I wonder if he did owe them money,' said Robert, expressing everyone's thoughts out loud.

'If those men hang around we may yet find out,' suggested James, 'and I think it would be unwise of any of us to walk about on our own.'

'What if they find out where we live? Would Pa be in danger?'

'I think, William, if they meet your Pa and see how he is they will see that he is as much a victim as they are.' Robert moved towards the bar. 'And I think we all need another drink.' He placed a florin on the bar. 'Pints all round please,' he nodded at the barman, 'and one for you. Thank you for your support.' All the other Spandlers murmured their agreement.

Later Robert and James left with the younger Robert. Henry and William, having a longer walk home, decided to use the privy first. They went into the yard together.

'That's strange,' said William as they stood urinating together, 'this wall is warm.'

'Think about it, Will,' laughed Henry. 'What's next door?'

'Of course, the yard. Bessie and the furnace. Can't think why I didn't realise that!'

They left and were only a few yards from the door of the King's arms when the men appeared and the one that had tried to punch William earlier now succeeded. The bigger man went for Henry and lifted him off his feet, pushing him up against the wall.

'Now tell us where Henry Spandler is,' he shouted.

'You're speaking to him.' Henry gasped as the man lifted him and thumped him into the wall again.

'Not you. You know who we want. We want our money,' the man demanded. However just then the door to Spandler's millwright's yard burst open and Robert and James appeared. The men, now outnumbered, ran off. Everyone breathed heavily for a few minutes while the sound of their footsteps faded away.

'Do you still think Pa is not in danger?' spluttered William.

'We'll talk about it in the morning. For now they've gone that way,' said Henry, pointing into town, 'so if we go home now we shouldn't meet them again tonight.'

'There was only two of them that time,' said William as they turned into Garrison Walk, 'I wonder where the little one went.' Henry did not reply.

They had been back ten minutes when there was a knock at the door. Eliza went to answer it but Henry stopped her. Henry and William went to the door together. Outside, several paces away from the front door, stood the smallest of the three men. For a few moments no-one spoke.

'Please sirs. Please can I speak with your father. I saw you get hurt and I'm sorry. I left when they said what they were going to do but then I came back and found a place to hide where I could see.'

'What? Watch the fun,' growled William but Henry put up his hand towards him and he was quiet.

'Your father was always a good man to work with, which is why we believed we'd be paid and carried on working when he left. I want to know what really happened.'

'How do we know we can trust you? Perhaps you have a knife up your sleeve.' The man took his jacket off and then started to undo his trousers.

'I'll take my clothes off and come in naked if that's what it takes.' Henry and William looked at each other and they both burst out laughing.

'That won't be necessary.' The man came to the door and suddenly Henry grabbed him. His eyes widened. William felt through his clothes, nodded and Henry let him go.

'Sorry about that but after this,' William pointed to his swollen eye, 'we just wanted to be sure.' The man shook himself.

'I think I understand,' he said, holding out his open hand. 'George Dunn.' Henry grasped the hand.

'It is good to meet you properly,' he said, 'and this is my brother William.' William and George also shook hands and everyone was smiling. Henry was wondering if now he might understand more fully what his father had done in London.

The man followed them indoors. He looked round the room and saw two young women sitting on one side of the fire, sewing, and an old couple next to them cradling a young child. On the floor next to the bed two children played and at the table an older girl was breaking up some bread into a bowl. The man looked confused and turned to Henry and William. They pointed to the man by the fire and George's eyes widened again.

'Henry, er, Mr Spandler sir?' he inquired. Henry watched his father look up and saw that he recognised him.

'George – so it didn't work out well for you either?' his father asked and then lapsed into silence for a few minutes before continuing, 'after what happened to me I didn't think the promises that had been made to me about my men would have been kept. I sold the business because I had to come back to my family here. I'd left them suddenly and I'd promised to return.' George frowned slightly as if he was trying to understand. Henry Spandler looked down at the floor and shook his head. 'He seemed a good man, the buyer. Jack introduced us and I'd known Jack for months and trusted him, but I think I was a fool. He spoke enthusiastically about the business and offered me more than it was worth. Talked about his plans to make the business bigger and how well you would all do from it.'

'But what happened to you,' interrupted George, pointing at Henry's misshapen arm.'

'I couldn't see beyond the large amount of money he was offering me – but the only reason it was so much was that he knew he was going to get it back and still have my business. I spent four months in hospital – nearly died. When I came out I spent a few days looking for him – for you as well

– but in the end I came back here. It took me months because I cannot walk very well as they'd also broken my leg.' The man frowned and looked down at his leg but Henry continued, 'I suppose you could say that it mended but it's not much good for walking on.'

'Jack told us that you had gone home to get more money and when you returned we would be paid.'

Henry shook his head. 'He seemed a good man but he has lied to us all.'

'And these are your sons.' George turned to Henry and William. 'You spoke a great deal about Henry, your eldest, and I see his brother is as good as he is. I always said that I thought something must have happened to you. I will find Jed and John and tell them and persuade them to return to London.'

'If they have lost their anger when you tell them the story then bring them to our family's millwrights' yard.' George smiled at the younger Henry's words. 'Our uncles would like to meet you properly and hear the story from you. I cannot promise anything because you'll understand that I am only employed there. But they own the business and may be able to help you.'

'Your father talked about the yard and I would like to see it. I will come.'

A week passed. Henry thought he saw the three men disappearing into Row Two when he came out of the yard after work one afternoon and another day when Eliza and Mary came back from the silk factory they saw George Dunn in the churchyard.

'We ought to call the constable,' William said after the girls had reported their sighting.

'He was very civil though,' said Eliza, 'raised his cap to us. And he was gentle with Pa that evening. I don't think he's a threat.'

'I still remember that thump!' declared William.

'I don't think the Constable could do much,' said Henry. 'He can't force them out of town for one thump and a threat.'

'So, we have to wait until one of us is hurt by them!'

'I don't believe that will happen. Remember Pa hired them in London so he must have thought they were good men.'

'Yes and remember Pa was tricked and attacked,' countered William, 'for all we know those other two were his attackers.'

'Those men were wronged just as much as Pa was. They may yet come to the yard and we'll learn some more. We'll not tell the Constable.' Henry had not raised his voice. William's frown indicated his disagreement with the decision but the authority with which Henry spoke silenced them all.

It was three days later that all three men, looking clean and sober, came to the yard.

'So, you see, we worked for no money for six weeks after he left because he'd always been a fair employer and we trusted him. We didn't know that he had been robbed and hurt.' George had told the tale again to Robert and James. He pointed to his two companions. 'These men have wives and children who are even now in the workhouse. It was bad enough for me to have been cheated but at least I do not have those who depend upon me.'

'Do you think your Pa would come if I sent the cart for him?' Robert asked Henry.

'He might if I go and take George with me,' replied Henry. Robert nodded and the two men left. When they returned Henry watched his father with the men he had employed and listened to what they said without saying much himself. He noted however that they all mentioned how proudly his father had spoken about him when he was away. Suddenly, standing next to his father in the yard where he enjoyed his daily toil, he was overcome with sadness for the loss of the man he had known when he was younger.

'What will you do now?' Robert asked the men. Henry brought his attention back to what was happening in front of him.

'We'll make our way home in the next day or two. We've had casual work down on the docks for the last few weeks but that has finished now. We need to start the walk while the weather is good.

Robert reached into his jacket pocket. 'These are for you,' he said, handing them a guinea each. 'I know that it will not replace all the money you should have received as wages. I will also come down to the stage and pay for your passage so that you can return to your families.'

'Y-y-you're going to pay for us to ride home!' George's voice betrayed his emotion. 'That young man was wrong that evening. You are a very generous family. You were a good man to work for,' he said to Henry, 'and I'm sorry that it all went wrong for you.'

'Yes, and I'm sorry that that young man made this all so difficult,' said Robert looking round for Edmund who had disappeared again. 'He is my son and does not always do the right thing.'

As summer turned to autumn Henry found less angst at home: his father had suddenly become frailer and was coughing a great deal although had become easier to live with. Henry was unsure whether meeting with his men had changed his father or if he was too ill to care. His mother became less anxious as his father mellowed and this cheered him. The only sadness was that Elizabeth was by now very ill. She did not cry tears and her cough became worse, sometimes causing her to vomit blood. She often sat on her father's knee, sharing a bowl into which they spat blood-stained mucus together.

In the new year Mary-Ann cried for her child, calling out her name as she stood and watched the coffin, which father and daughter shared, going down into the grave. After this she became very confused: sometimes she would ask Caroline where her husband was; other days she would say he was away working on a mill; then she would remember that he had gone to London and would ask Henry when he would be home. A week after he was buried she suddenly turned to Eliza and asked her if she knew whether her Henny had been in the coffin with Elizabeth. When Eliza nodded she set her chair rocking and cried for him.

10

'They say the water covers the jetty!' exclaimed Henry one morning. 'I'm going to see. Are you coming?'

William shrugged his shoulders. 'I've seen the sea many times and it's wet and windy. I'd rather stay here by the fire.' He was sitting in the chair that had been his father's and which he and Henry used now.

'Come on. It's always fun to watch the fools that try to play with the waves.' Eliza and Mary looked at each other and shook their heads.

William scowled. 'I'm not coming. Why do you want to see people risking their lives for some fun?'

'I remember you laughing at their antics when you were younger.'

'I knew nothing of life then – or death.' William turned from Henry and folded his arms. Henry shrugged, picked up his coat and left. He walked through Market Place and along King Street. As he turned down Jetty Road towards the sea he had to fight the wind which took his breath away. However his stride was strong and soon he came to the Bath House. He took shelter in the doorway and watched the waves until it was time to leave for his day's work at the yard. The sight of the spray leaping up into the air delighted him even though, like William, he had seen it many times before. It was too rough that day for the fools but he was quite pleased that there was no-one there, having only made the comment to encourage William, who had been morose since their father's death, to come with him. He enjoyed the solitude and the energy of the waves invigorated him. He stood until the cold penetrated his shoes and then turned back: with the wind behind him he made his way to the yard.

The men were standing around the boiler supping tankards of tea before they started the day's work. He joined them and found they were talking about the sea.

'Old Ned said that it will get worse. He's expecting a storm surge. Says the sea might breach the river over South Denes.'

'I heard yesterday that the landlord of the Holkham Tavern is moving anything that's not fixed to a warehouse further back.'

'Going to be bad then. The river will rise as well - flood the cesspits under the houses at the bottom end of the Rows.'

'So those rich merchants on South Quay will get something of the stink!' Everyone laughed and Henry remembered Genevieve and her family. By now he'd seen her many times with her mother: noticing how they simpered together he realised how fortunate he'd been to be rejected. He smiled at the thought of their discomfiture.

'The drain is almost full,' observed William as they walked home down Garrison Walk that evening.

'Mmm, so long as it does not overflow we're better off because it's moving quickly and taking the foul air with it,' replied Henry.

'Oh,' shrugged William, 'it'll probably spill over into our cottage tomorrow.' He kicked at a stone as he walked. 'It always works out badly for us. It'll be fine for Edmund – have you seen him strutting about the yard since young Robert went to sea? Misfortune never seems to come to that stripling. They'll all be high and dry in the cottage at the yard. Not us, things go wrong for us and we work hard for them.'

'And get paid well for it.' Henry glanced at his brother. 'Remember you won't receive half what you get as an apprentice elsewhere.' Although he tried to encourage him, William's gloom affected Henry and he became silent. He thought of his father and it was as if he'd been two people. He grieved for the man he'd respected through his childhood but the man who'd destroyed his future had replaced that grief with ire.

The following day the storm coincided with a high spring tide. The front wall of Holkham Tavern was demolished by the force of the water as were many other properties on the seafront. In two of the mills on the Denes the millers, being unwilling to stop milling, had not locked the sails early enough so that the wind had spun the cap and turned the sails backwards, damaging the cogs. They had been fortunate in that they had managed to uncouple the millstones thus avoiding the generation of heat that would have led to an explosion and the destruction of the mill. As it was they would lose several days earnings whilst having to pay for the skills of Spandler's millwrights. Henry was pleased because he could show Jim how the backwards turning of the mill had changed the shape of the cogs. This would demonstrate how any malformed cogs in a mill would be found by the wind when it turned the sails and forced into the shape it demanded, resulting in vibrations and noise. He knew that the quality of a mill was apparent through the smoothness of its action. This repair would teach Jim, better than any words, how important it was for each cog to be shaped correctly: Jim would learn that it was the wind that was truly the master of their craft and their skill was merely one of harnessing its power.

Six weeks later the weather had changed again. Henry arrived home to find Mary-Ann and Caroline sitting in the spring sunshine in the yard.

'It's good to see you outside, Ma.'

'Eliza suggested it last night,' said Caroline. 'She'd called in at Owle's, the chemist, for some linctus for us and he said that he'd read that the doctors in London say that fresh air could be a cure. He said that they were saying that you should be outside as much as possible during the day. We thought we'd try it but it's getting cold now so I think we'll come in.'

'Where's William?' Mary-Ann asked.

'Gone for a drink with young Jim. It might make his temper sweeter,' replied Henry.

'Or not if he has too many. Perhaps you should have stayed with him,' said Caroline as she helped Mary-Ann to her feet.

'I think the uncles will be there. I wanted to see how you two were today.'

'The fresh air has improved my appetite – that fish stew smells good,' Mary-Ann exclaimed. Henry allowed her to lean on his arm as she started coughing. She was so frail that it almost felt to him as if a bird had landed on his arm but she smiled at him and her eyes were bright. On some days it appeared that his mother was at last regaining her wits and he wondered whether there was any link between the return of his mother's mind and the death of his father. However, on other days, her breathing was laboured and she became easily confused. The London doctors may be right and the consumption that took his sisters may yet spare his mother and Caroline – but he couldn't really believe it.

'They say the bellman's been out,' said Mary one evening in June as she and Eliza came in from the silk factory.

'Yes.' William stood up and looked in the bread tin on the shelves but it was empty. He was hungry and, although Caroline had prepared some vegetables, she had been too tired to start cooking. He sighed: it would be a while before the evening meal was ready. He turned back to Mary. 'There was a notice on the door of the Angel and they're going to take down the Market Cross.'

'I see,' she said as she lifted the cloth that covered the water bucket under the sink, 'and I also see that you should have fetched water from the pump when you came in.'

'Ma did you hear that?' Caroline was sitting by the fire with her mother. She nudged her and pointed to William.

'They're going to take down the Market Cross,' William repeated, raising his voice slightly and looking at Mary-Ann.

She shook her head. 'But it's been there for lifetimes! I remember my Henry saying that he was told by his father that they whipped miscreants by the cross when he was young.'

'I expect many of the older people in the town will wonder why it's necessary to take it down,' suggested William.

'Are you still here?' Mary laughed. 'I cannot cook these taters without water. I thought you were hungr...' The door banged as William left the house with the bucket.

A fortnight passed. Henry was at the yard.

'It's being sold by auction next week. I think I'll attend,' Robert was saying.

'You're not thinking of buying the Market Cross!' exclaimed Henry. 'What would you do with it?'

Robert chuckled. 'No, I'm just interested. I wonder how much it's worth.'

'Much of what is old in the town has gone.' James shook his head. 'North and South gates when we were children and now the Market Cross. It'll be St Nicholas's next!' They all laughed at the idea that someone might buy their parish church, the largest in all England, and move it elsewhere. A few weeks later the townsfolk were commenting on the strangeness of the appearance of Market Place without the Cross and Robert reported back that it had been sold for fifty-five pounds and six shillings: the purchaser's identity had been concealed.

There had been some heat in August but now September had arrived and the easterly wind had an edge to it. Henry pulled his jacket together as he walked along North Road to the yard. William accompanied him but they did not speak that morning: Henry was occupied with thoughts of what the day would bring and William was quiet. As Henry put his hand on the door of the yard he briefly wondered at William's silence but the thought was pushed away by the sight of the young man standing with Jim. It was Jim's brother Frederick, known to the family as Freddie. The previous evening his father James had complimented Henry on the training his eldest son was receiving and had asked him if he could also take Freddie on as an apprentice. Henry agreed but his enthusiasm was tempered by the strangeness of his young cousin, who, as a crawling babe, had come close to the fire just as hot coals fell out. They'd landed on his face and he'd lost his left eye: the wound, as it healed, had pulled up that side of his mouth into a permanent grin. Overnight he had wondered about that missing eye and how it would affect his ability to measure distances and angles: it would make training him much more difficult. However if he was as quick witted as his brother it would not be impossible. It occurred to him that if it had happened to Edmund, whose mind was slow, he would be quite incapable.

Jim, his first apprentice, was doing well and Henry respected his intelligence. He looked at him and Jim met his gaze and then looked at his brother. He turned back to Henry and nodded, which Henry took to be an indication of his support. He was encouraged by this because Jim would know his brother's disability and the skills that he would need. He began, as with all the apprentices, by handing him a besom and telling him to sweep the yard, which was strewn with the wood shavings and sawdust that was the inevitable waste that their craft produced. Freddie grinned at his brother, before setting to work, and Henry guessed he had been forewarned. He looked over to Edmund who was nudging William and pulling a face with one eye shut. In a moment Henry was standing very close to him.

'He may look strange but he's willing to work,' he hissed in his ear, 'which is more than I remember you being.' Henry recalled the day, before his father went to London, when Edmund had started as an apprentice. It was the same day as William and they'd been set to work together. Edmund, knowing that his father was working away, had refused to sweep and had even shouted and stamped his foot when

Henry's father and James had tried to insist. Now Henry spoke loudly, deliberately, so that everyone could hear.

'Hard work is far more valuable than appearance in the business of being a millwright.' Edmund, who was often preening himself, flushed. Everyone smiled. Freddie, however, ignored them all as he worked the shavings out from under the lathe.

Henry returned home alone that night because William had gone into Market Place to the cobblers. Small repairs, such as soling and heeling, he did himself but this time he decided that he had patched his shoes too many times and that he needed to have the whole of the bottom of the shoe replaced. He'd considered trying to do it himself but decided that he would probably be walking more comfortably if he paid a craftsman whose skill it was. A friend of his whom he'd known since he was at school was from a family of cobblers and William told Henry that he would wait at the shop whilst they were repaired and then he was going to partake of the food at the Angel Inn with his friend.

That day Aunt Hannah, with whom Rachel lived, had invited Eliza and Mary to spend the evening with them. Consequently Henry found himself at home with just Caroline and his mother. As he entered Caroline pointed to the fire upon which was a pan of water. The evening meal was on a plate on top of the pan with another plate on top.

'Fried fish,' said Caroline. 'Eliza cooked it for us before they left because the smoke from the frying was making me cough and I couldn't do it. There's mashed swede in the bowl next to the fire there as well.' Henry brought all the food over to the chairs by the fire and allowed his mother and sister to take what they wanted, finishing the rest himself.

'How have you both been today?' he asked as he swallowed the last mouthful.

'We spent a few hours outside but it was cold.'

'I think you both seem to be better for spending as much time as you have outside this summer. It's a pity it seems to be coming to an end early.' They sat in companionable silence for considerable time. Then Mary-Ann started agitating her chair. Henry and Caroline looked at each other as she also started whining.

'My babies, my babies have gone.' She repeated the phrase over and over whilst she moved the chair faster and faster. Her whining became louder. Then she turned on Henry, 'I had them inside me. I gave them life. But they've gone, they've gone.' She drew from her apron pocket a crumpled piece of paper. 'You didn't take care of them like he said.' As she opened it up Henry felt as if a hole was opening for him to fall into. It was the letter his father had written before he went to London. She still had it!

'Ma, Henry tried his best,' said Caroline gently. 'They've not all gone – Rachel is at Aunt Hannah's with Tom and Martha. Eliza and Mary have grown into fine young women. William works at the yard with Henry.'

'But the others, the little ones, my babies!' Mary-Ann wailed. Caroline hugged her whilst Henry shook his head.

'You cannot blame Henry, Ma. He's worked hard to support us. Pa should never have gone.'

'Your Pa was doing what he thought was the best for his family. He was a good man.'

'I know that Ma,' said Henry, his voice even and controlled, 'but it was because he went we had to stay here in Garrison Walk. It's the bad air here that took your children. If he had not gone we'd be living at the yard now.'

'Yes but he told you to look after us.' Mary-Ann screeched as she waved the paper in front of his face.

Henry stood up. 'I'm going out.' Caroline nodded to him whilst she held her mother tighter to stop her arms flailing.

It was during that night Henry first had the dream. He was standing next to his father's grave as the coffin was lowered but the lid had not been fixed and he could see his father's body. Suddenly his father sat up with Elizabeth in his arms. In her hand was the letter. They faded from view and the coffin was empty but then another body began to appear. Henry woke and a tearless sob caught in the back of his throat. For a few moments he breathed rapidly. His eyes were wide and staring as he tried to see something that would explain his dream. Then his muscles tightened, curling him into a rigid ball. His face buried itself in the pillow. When he uncurled some time later he was unsure how much time had passed. Had he slept again? His head hurt and his throat was sore with dryness. He shook himself and pushed his thoughts towards Freddie and the yard in order to leave the night and its companions behind. However he was not very successful because whenever he was quiet he could see that coffin again. His apprentices found him to be uncharacteristically irritable that day. He dreaded returning home that night but when he did so his mother was happy and laughing, telling him what a wonderful son he was. Caroline commented on the contrast with the evening before. Henry shrugged: his mother had brought forth ghosts into his dreams and he doubted that a few compliments would banish them.

There was no late summer that year. Instead, by the end of October, it was windy and cold and some said that they were expecting early snow. At the yard Robert, as the head of the business, decided it was time to lift the gloom that seemed to have settled. He announced that after work was finished that Friday night chestnuts would be roasted on shovels in Bessie's furnace and he would ask at the King's Arms for them to send some ale.

Henry enjoyed that evening as he sat with his uncles. They talked about the millwright's craft which was the interest that they had in common. It was not only a source of income but the thing which occupied their thoughts through most of the day and was very important to all of them. They continually talked through better ways of doing things and that evening was no exception: James shared a new technique he had developed for the complicated task of lifting a new sail-arm into position. As usual, in that company, Henry relaxed and laughed as he joined in the conversation with the older men. The dream lurked, almost forgotten, in the back of his mind until the ale concealed it completely leaving Henry free to enjoy himself.

Across the yard from Henry, Edmund was sitting on one of the benches. He was leaning backwards, supported by the edge of the workbench behind him, with the ankle of his right leg resting on his left. In that position the tightness of his trousers bore witness to his mother's cooking. In spite of the coolness of the day his chubby, childlike face was shiny with perspiration whilst his hands moved almost as rapidly as his tongue. William, the person to whom Edmund spoke, was flicking his eyes between Edmund and the area behind him, where his other cousins, Jim and Freddie, were sitting together. Eventually William stood and made to move off towards them.

'Don't like my company then?' Edmund's voice was staccato with hurt.

'Actually no, not much.' William walked away. Edmund stood up as if to follow him but then sat down, breathing heavily. After a few minutes he stood again and moved slowly to where Robert, his father, was sitting with James and Henry. Robert had been watching him and, as he approached, he could see his pallor and the bead of sweat on the end of his nose.

'You're not joining in the fun with your cousins then?' Robert asked, nodding in the direction of Jim and Freddie who had just roared with laughter.

'Pa, I'm not well,' he bleated as his breathing quickened again and he held onto the end of a lathe. 'I'm going indoors.' Robert shook his head as his son moved slowly across the yard to the cottage.

'He does look ill,' ventured James.

Robert nodded. 'His mother is convinced there is actually something wrong. The doctors say it may be his heart – however I wonder if it's in his head. This happens whenever he is in a situation that he cannot control. Will has just left him on his own and moved over to join Jim and Freddie.'

It was Henry's turn to nod. 'Yes, and you know I sometimes think that, because you are the most senior millwright and he is your son, then he thinks we all ought to want to hear what he has to say and enjoy being in his company. He considers himself important.'

11

'How's your Ma?' Robert asked one morning, 'and your sister?'

'They've both recovered somewhat this year. They've been sitting outside as much as possible and now neither of them coughs as badly as they used to – it fact it's now twelve months since Caroline coughed up blood – unless, of course, it's happening when I am here and she's not telling me. I saw it a great deal last year.'

'Perhaps she is on the mend. Maybe they both are,' James suggested. Henry looked from one to the other of his uncles and smiled a little.

'You may be right. I just hope the winter is not too hard on them. Caroline says that when it is dry, even if it is cold, they'll still sit outside – just wear lots of clothes.'

As he was returning home Henry thought about Edmund and what would happen if he did have a bad heart and pre-deceased his father. He knew that Edmund's elder brother, Robert, had gone to sea and, although there was a younger brother, he wondered about the future of the yard and how it would include himself.

A few days later Hannah, James's wife, called at the cottage in Garrison Walk.

'These are for you,' she said to Mary-Ann and Caroline as she handed them a parcel wrapped in brown paper and tied with string. 'James told me that you are trying to sit outside as much as possible and that that is helping your coughs. I thought that these might keep you warm.'

'B-But they're lovely,' stammered Caroline as she undid the string and opened the parcel. Mary-Ann unfolded the blanket which was on top.

'They look new,' she stated, gazing at Hannah in amazement.

'They are. James bought them from one of the merchants on South Quay last week because he liked the pattern on them – but really we have no need of more blankets.'

Caroline had passed the top blanket to her mother and now unfolded the second one onto her own lap. She stroked it and traced the pattern with her finger before looking at Hannah. 'It's beautiful,' she whispered.

Hannah nodded. 'Yes they both are – and I think you need beautiful things when you are unwell. It helps you feel better.' Caroline and Mary-Ann beamed at each other.

'Thank-you,' they said together.

December approached and Henry's mood lightened. For the first time in years he was looking forward to the Christmas celebration at the yard. His mother and sister continued to improve and he was no longer plagued by dreams. Caroline was well enough to venture out to the market and Mary-Ann had become loving and caring again, more like the mother he remembered from his childhood. Those London doctors might be right. Perhaps they will beat the wasting disease.

In January it was very cold and water on the surface of the marshes near Yarmouth froze. At the yard William had discovered that he had an aptitude towards iron moulding. He had recently finished his apprenticeship and was encouraged to think of ways of expanding the business. He designed ice blades that could be strapped on over a pair of shoes. These he made from the waste iron that was now of too poor a quality to be used in a mill. He sold them on the market. Robert was pleased and allowed him to keep two pairs for himself.

'Here you are,' he said to Henry as they left the yard, 'this pair's for you. If this freeze continues we could go and try them out.' Henry didn't much like skating because he usually ended up falling over all the time but he grinned at his brother. It was good to see him happy.

'Thank you. It's going dark now and I'm tired. We're both off work on Saturday afternoon. Shall we try them then?' William nodded. They were just approaching the turning for Garrison Walk when a cart passed them.

'Look at that cart!' exclaimed William, 'it's far too full.' Henry looked up to see the cart turn into Garrison Walk.

'The drain must have frozen so they're taking the waste to the river in carts like they used to. You're right, it is too full. That bit's hanging over the side.' They followed the cart. As they turned the corner they saw the flaccid length of intestine fall from the cart not far from their front door. Before they went indoors they moved it into the frozen drain with their feet, retching as they did so.

It was late on Friday afternoon. Work at the yard had finished and it was dark outside.

'Henry and I are going skating on the ice tomorrow,' William was telling Jim and Freddie. 'Meet us at the suspension bridge at one o'clock if you've finished here by then. Otherwise we'll be on the marsh to the right of the bridge.'

Freddie and Jim nodded enthusiastically. 'We know – Henry told us,' Jim informed him and then continued. 'We're going to stay behind now and do as much clearing up as we can tonight.'

'Where's Ed?' asked Henry as he approached them. 'We can't really ask you to join us without asking him. After all he's our cousin as well.'

'He went into the cottage about half an hour ago,' said Freddie.

Henry walked over to the cottage. Just inside the door, in the office, Robert was working at a ledger. Henry tapped on the door.

'May I pass through?' he asked, 'I want to speak with Edmund.' Robert raised his eyebrows. 'We're going skating

tomorrow afternoon. I like to ask him if he wishes to join us.'
Robert shook his head.

'I doubt it. Yes, come through. He's in the parlour with his mother.'

Henry now tapped on the parlour door. Mary, Robert's wife, looked up.

'Hello Henry,' she said without smiling, her eyes returning to her son. Edmund was lying back in a chair, his head lolling to one side while his breath crackled. 'This is what he is like after a day working in the yard. I keep telling Robert that he is not well, that he shouldn't work him so hard.' Mary looked up at Henry again. As she did so Edmund raised his head from the back of the chair and winked. Henry, with difficulty, controlled his surprise.

'I came to tell Edmund that we are going skating tomorrow and to ask if he wished to accompany us.' Edmund looked delighted at the invitation but Henry continued before he suddenly recovered. 'However, I think I can see that he will not be able to come.'

'That is right,' replied Mary, 'my poor boy. He works hard in the yard and then does not have the energy to enjoy himself.'

'I am sorry that he is unwell. I will leave you to care for him. Good-day.'

'Good-day to you. Thank you for coming to ask him.' As Henry left Edmund lifted a fat hand in farewell.

On the ice the following day Henry discovered that he wasn't the only one to struggle with staying on his feet. He and Freddie spent a lot of time helping each other to stand whilst William and Jim skated so well that they even tried doing some tricks. They received a round of applause from a group of young girls who were also on the ice. Henry shook his head.

'Why are their fathers allowing them to come and skate as if they were boys? They should be at home by the fire with their mothers.'

Freddie laughed. 'That is the sort of thing our grandfather would have said! I don't see why they should not enjoy this just as much as us.'

At the end of the afternoon they all walked together through George street, over White Horse Plain and past the yard. The cottage where Jim and Freddie lived was a little way down Caister Road so they split up when they reached the corner of Garrison Walk.

'I enjoyed this afternoon,' said William as Henry and he walked towards the cottage.

'Yes I can see that,' replied Henry. 'I'm pleased. You've seemed happier lately.'

William nodded. 'Yes, I think it's because things seem to be going right for us now. Ma and Caroline are recovering. I've passed my apprenticeship. Perhaps we can think about moving to something better than this now that I am earning more.' He jerked his head towards the cottage and over to the drain.

Henry shrugged. 'Perhaps,' was all he said as they reached their front door and went inside.

February and March gave way to April. It was the end of the working day and when Henry walked home that evening the sun was shining. Several people that he'd passed had smiled and Henry had reciprocated so that, by the time he'd reached the cottage, he was in high spirits.

He opened the door and, for a moment, his brain could not comprehend the scene before him. He was unable to move. His mother was in her chair but only just and Caroline was crouched alongside the chair trying to prevent her falling onto the floor. Blood streamed from Mary-Ann's mouth. She coughed and gurgled in an attempt to breathe while her eyes stared at him, unseeing. Then this grotesque statue, which was his mother and sister, started to fall: the movement unlocked him. He sprang over to them and lifted Mary-Ann from on top of Caroline.

'It's alright, I have her,' he cried out. Caroline did not answer but fell sideways. It was then that he realised that the blood was not all from his mother. He carried his mother over to the bed and laid her down and was just picking Caroline up from the floor when the door opened. For a few seconds there was silence, then William screamed.

'No!' He threw his hands above his head, staring at the ceiling whilst he hammered either side of the doorframe with his fists. 'No!' Abruptly he stopped hammering and looked down again, his head still and his eyes swivelling round the room. He looked from the pool of blood by the fire to his brother as Henry laid Caroline next to her mother. Henry stroked Caroline's head whilst her eyes moved from her mother to William.

'Go and meet Mary and Eliza. Prepare them, tell them what's happened.'

'Ma?' William's voice faltered.

Henry looked at him. 'She's dead.' William's whole body shook as if Henry had struck him. Then he turned and ran from the cottage, banging the door behind him. Henry continued to stroke Caroline with one hand whilst he pulled the bench towards him. He was aware that his legs were shaking beyond his control. He sat down so that his head was nearer to Caroline's. When he spoke his voice was soft and quiet.

'I thought you were both recovering,' he said whilst his eyes moved from Caroline to her mother and back again.

'We've been coughing again the last few weeks,' she whispered, 'not much, until yesterday. Ma coughed blood then but I caught it in a bowl and cleaned her up. I didn't want to worry you.' Caroline stopped and her head flopped sideways.

'And what about you?' Caroline did not reply and Henry continued, 'Ma is gone. You heard me tell William?' Caroline's eyes were closed. 'You helped her until the end, Caroline. I will always remember you for that. When I have my children my first girl will be called Caroline because I will want her to be as special as you are.' He was not sure if she heard but he thought he saw the tiniest of smiles on her lips.

Caroline outlived her mother by three days and they shared a funeral. When Sarah had died at the same time as her father they had shared a coffin but at seventeen Caroline was considered too old: they were buried separately.

The day after the funeral Robert and James came to the cottage in Garrison Walk.

'It is not right that Mary and Eliza live with you,' said Robert to Henry and William, 'not now that you are alone.'

'Say it, Uncle Robert,' William muttered through clenched teeth, 'you mean, now that our mother is dead as well as our father. He killed her you know, as much as if he'd done it with his own hands.'

'William.' Henry put a hand on his arm but he brushed it away. 'William you must not talk like that. It does not help us.' William shrugged but said no more. Henry turned to his uncles. 'What do you suggest that we do?'

'Our sister Hannah is unwell and, even with Rachel's help, is struggling with the younger ones,' explained Robert. 'I think, if Eliza comes with them, they could both come to live with us. Hannah is quite happy for Rachel to continue to stay and even for Mary to come with her.'

'So Tom and Martha will be at your house with Eliza. Mary and Rachel will be together at Aunt Hannah's,' repeated Henry. He looked at William as he spoke. 'What of us?'

'You can stay together or go your separate ways. You are men now and able to support yourselves although I should be glad if you did not go far. I would like you to continue as millwrights at the yard.' The girls had listened to the conversation. Mary brushed away a tear.

'We will not be far away and I'm sure our uncles will be pleased for you to come and call on us,' she said as she looked from one to the other of them. Robert and James nodded and she continued. 'Please let us have one more evening together as brothers and sisters in our parents' home. Eliza and I will collect up our belongings tonight and the boys can accompany us to our new homes when we all finish work tomorrow.'

Henry and William stayed in Garrison Walk. Henry did suggest they looked for somewhere else but William just shrugged his shoulders.

It was three weeks later when Robert took Edmund and William with him to inspect a mill which the owner said was not turning into the wind properly.

'Edmund,' Robert said to his son, 'I want you to climb up to the cap and make an assessment. Take the rope up with you and when you get to the top tie the end securely and let it drop down here. We'll attach the basket with the tools and you can pull it up. We'll follow them and I expect you to have decided what needs to be done by the time we join you.' Edmund pulled a face and ambled off up the stairs inside the mill. 'Move quicker than that. We want to finish this job today,' Robert barked.

'He is going a little bit faster – I think,' William observed.

'I'm going as fast as I can,' called down Edmund from the first landing. Robert shook his head.

Edmund continued to climb and, in the silence of the mill, his breathing became louder and faster. Robert paced the floor until, eventually, the end of the rope appeared and they could tie on the basket and follow him up the stairs.

When Robert and William reached the small platform at the top of the mill, they found Edmund slumped on the floor, his face red and shiny. His mouth was open and he was still out of breath. William took the end of the rope from his hand hauled up the tools.

'Look at you – still panting,' said Robert. 'This is our craft, my son. You need to be able to do this. Perhaps if you weren't so fat? I wouldn't like to carry your weight up the stairs, which is why we use the rope for the tools. Now, have you worked out what is wrong with this cap?'

Edmund shook his head. 'I can't see anything.'

'Have you been outside?' Robert nodded towards the small door in the side of the cap that opened onto an inspection ledge. Edmund shook his head again.

'Robert, I'll go,' offered William. He bent down and opened the door. The wind gusted through the space.

'The wind's risen in the last hour,' observed Robert. William poked his head out into the space. He pulled hard at one of the rings on the side of the cap before turning back to Robert.

'The rings seem strong so I'll have something to hold on to. There weren't any at that one last week.'

'Yes I heard about that. You should have waited for ropes.'

William shrugged. 'I'm just taking a quick look now. The rings will be enough. He moved out onto the ledge which was barely wider than the length of his feet. He moved round the cap towards the cap sail and leant out at an angle to see more easily. Suddenly the ring that he was holding pulled out of the cap. Robert heard it. His eyes widened. He looked out. William was wobbling, trying to regain his balance. Robert reached out to him but he was too far away. As he fell he yelled for his father as a young lad might cry out when taking a tumble but his father was dead and no-one could help him. Robert raced down the stairs and out of the mill where William's body lay in an inhuman shape.

'Will!' he shouted. Robert looked into his eyes but they were blank. His leg twitched and he shuddered as his life ended.

'He died just as I reached him but I don't think he knew I was there,' explained Robert, later, to Henry.

'Why did he go out onto the cap without roping himself first? That's what we always do.'

'I know, and I should have stopped him. He said the rings were strong. He was just taking a quick look to see what the problem was. Do you know he went out and worked without ropes last week as well? It was a calm day apparently. He took a risk then.'

Henry nodded. 'He's been ill-tempered and gloomy since Ma and Caroline died.'

'Go to the factory and ask to see the girls,' suggested Robert. Henry shook his head.

'I'll go after I've finished here. Bad news can wait.' He continued to work that afternoon, calmly, as if nothing of importance had happened. His composure lasted until later that evening after he'd seen his other siblings and returned to Garrison Walk. Then he ran around bawling and thumping the walls.

That night he dreamt. This time he saw not just his father but his mother and departed siblings. They all sat up one after the other and held their hands out to him before disappearing through the bottom of the coffin. He woke the following morning unrested and knew, above all else, that he could not continue to live in Garrison Walk.

12

'The King is dead! Long live the Queen Victoria!' The town crier rang his bell and intoned the words. It was the twentieth of June 1837. As Henry left his lodgings he could hear the commotion of voices echoing the bellman's words to each other, spreading the news through the town. It was not long before he heard the news himself: a young boy, walking towards him, saw his look of inquiry.

'The King is dead! Long live Queen Victoria!' The boy took off his cap and nodded to Henry who doffed his in return and continued on his way to the yard. Death is something that comes whether you are King or the son of a millwright he mused. It had been three months since William's funeral. The hard edge to his grief was dulled a little but the anger was still there. It was exacerbated when he saw Edmund. As the eldest son of the millwright in charge (discounting Robert who had gone to sea) he occupied the position that would have been Henry's if his father had not sold his share in the yard when his grandfather died. Edmund was still only an apprentice but, when his father was not there, he acted as if he was already the master-in-charge. He was aware of Henry's misfortune and it seemed to Henry that he pointed it out whenever he could.

Henry arrived at the yard and could see, at the far end near Bessie the steam engine, a group of apprentices having their early tea. Some of them had already been out on a job and, although it was June, the early mornings were cold. Robert had introduced the tea when he first became master: he had memories of trying to work when he was cold and knew that this small consideration on his part would result in more work from his men. Edmund was standing with his back to the door, surrounded by the group. Henry had wondered why they were so inclined to stay in his company until it occurred to him that Edmund would be their future employer. He could often be seen standing in the middle of the group pontificating.

'I was there. I know what happened,' he was saying as Henry walked across from the door of the yard to the cottage, the front room of which was the office. He heard the latch go on the gate and turned around to see Robert following him. His uncle smiled and Henry was turning back to enter the office when Edmund spoke again in a loud voice.

'I tell you I was there. It was no accident – he deliberately let go and allowed himself to fall.' Henry stopped and turned around again. Robert was standing next to him, put one hand on his shoulder, a finger of the other hand to his lips and then pointed to the office.

'I was there. I'll deal with it,' he whispered as he propelled Henry into the office. James went to Henry, who had stopped just inside the door, and drew him towards the chair by the fire. Henry's legs were shaking and he sank into it as Edmund's voice carried across the yard.

'My father had told me to do the inspection and I was standing by the door to the cap as they came up the stairs. I really wanted to do it but he pushed me out of the way. Said he had something he had to do out there. Then the next thing we hear him screaming like a baby as he fell. I can't believe they buried him in the churchyard. He's damned and should not defile sanctified ground.' No-one asked him a question. They just stared. 'It's good that he's gone. This business can't support failures and I think it would be better if his broth...' The eyes of the group were no longer on him: they were looking behind him. He turned around to see his father standing there.

'Pa! I thought you were out!'

'So that you'd be safe with your lies! It would be bad enough for you to be talking ill of the dead if what you were saying was true. I was there and I know what happened,' Robert said as he glared at Edmund and then flicked his eyes over the group. 'I remember you slouched on the floor, breathless from walking up the stairs.' Someone giggled but Robert met his eyes and he was immediately quiet. 'William went out on that cap to do what you should have done. That you should suggest he took his own life sickens me. He was an excellent millwright and I was going to put one of you younger ones as his apprentice – you would have been taught well. Spandler's yard is poorer for our loss.' Robert fixed his gaze upon his son; his voice became quiet and his articulation very precise. 'This day I am ashamed to call you my son. You are so full of your own importance that you cannot see your faults. You are only an apprentice and you have a great deal more to learn, especially about yourself. Later I will be going out to a new water pump and I am taking two apprentices with me to dig the channel. You will be one of them and I shall ensure that you are the one who does the most unpleasant tasks. The least that you deserve is a day being wet, muddy and cold.' Edmund moved quickly across the yard, his fat, wobbling posterior producing smiles on the faces of the other apprentices. As he stormed through the office to go to his mother Henry made to rise but James pushed him back down and in a moment Edmund passed through and was gone. Robert entered the office.

'He's coming with me this afternoon whatever his mother says. He's a further shock coming because tonight I'm taking him to all his drinking places to set the story right.'

'It's sad but I wonder if he is right,' stated Henry. 'William had been morose since Ma and Caroline died.'

'Henry, have you forgotten that I was there?' Robert entreated. 'I was with him that morning. He was talking about the mill as we walked and was as irritated with Edmund as I was. He knew the job needed doing and that is why he went out there. I know he was sometimes careless for his own safety but I do not think he killed himself. The ring had come out from the cap and when I reached him on the ground his fist was still locked around it. No, ignore William and listen to me. He did not take his own life.' Robert was looking into

Henry's eyes as he spoke and for a few moments Henry stared at him. Then he nodded.

'Thank you.' He paused and drew breath. 'Thank you for saying that. I had had my doubts. Your words mean more than I can tell. I...I trust your judgement.' Henry's stutter betrayed his emotion.

'And now I'm going to prise my boy away from his Mama,' said Robert as he passed through the doorway leading into   the   parlour.

13

In Yarmouth the first Row, or very narrow street, was next to the old medieval walls of the town, and, because of this, had been given the name of Rampart Row. The ground sloped across the width of the Row from the town wall to the open drain that ran along its length. Houses had been built in the arches of the wall but the slope of the ground caused them to lean towards the centre of the row so that it had become necessary for support beams to be inserted between them and the backs of the buildings in Row Two. In one of these houses Henry now lodged: with only himself to support he was able to afford the best room in the house and it was upstairs at the front. From his window the tilt of the houses, which varied along the Row, together with the irregular angles of the beams, made a very odd picture: Henry, used to estimating angles and distances as part of his craft, was fascinated by them. In another room in the house the landlady served up meals. She also sold beer and cider, having taken advantage of the relaxation in the licensing laws. This suited Henry who would sit on his own and sup ale after he had eaten. He rarely went to the King's Arms now: socialising with his cousins tended to remind him of his loss and the disadvantage his father had put him in.

One day, towards the end of the summer, Robert came to Henry at the yard.

'Your Eliza requested to speak with me. She told me she is courting a young man and he came to see me last night. It is only right that you should meet him and I feel you will be pleased for her. He's coming to the cottage tomorrow evening and my Mary has decided that, whilst Eliza is twenty-five next week as well, we'll have some merry-making. I've sent a message to my sister Hannah to come with Mary and Rachel.' Robert was watching Henry's face carefully as he spoke but he need not have worried. Henry's eyes lit up and he smiled.

'That's very kind of you. We will be together again for the first time since…' Henry's voice faltered but he steadied himself, 'since William's funeral. To have cause to make merry is good for us all.'

'I wondered about asking James and Hannah and their family as well?' Henry nodded enthusiastically. James's eldest sons, Jim and Freddie, were his two apprentices and he liked their company.

'Your evening meal, Mr Spandler,' said Maria as she placed a plate of stew on the table in front of him later that evening.

'Maria, before I forget, I will not require a meal tomorrow. I am eating at the yard.'

'Your uncle looking after his workers again?' Maria enquired.

Henry shook his head. 'No, he's looking after his brother's family – that's my sisters and brothers and myself – as is right for the head of the family.' Maria raised her eyebrows and Henry continued, 'My elder sister is being courted by a tailor from Yorkshire and the family is gathering together to meet him.' Maria smiled. One evening a few months previously Henry, who had been tired and had had one too many tankards of Maria's ale, had shared with her his family's story. She was an older woman who had raised four children to adulthood and, although the lodging house was her business, she was also caring. Occasionally Henry wondered whether he had been wise but she had kept his story to herself and Henry felt comfortable with her.

'It is good that you gather for a happy occasion,' she commented. 'If you let me have your best clothes I will prepare them for you to change into tomorrow.'

The following day, after work, Henry returned to his lodgings. It was nearly the end of September and, although there was a chill in the air, he was sweaty and carried the smell of smoke from working with the fire for the steam engine. He knew Maria would have hot water ready for him to wash before he changed. Later, clean and refreshed, made his way back to the yard where Robert lived in the cottage. As he walked it occurred to him that it was almost a year since they'd had the chestnut evening and he remembered how William had enjoyed it. It would be this Christmas soon enough: last year his mother and Caroline were better than they'd been for a long time and he'd allowed himself to be happy. He stopped as disappointment hit him as it had done many times and his shoulders fell as he clenched his fists. After a few moments he looked up. Rampart Row was narrow and he could only see a thin strip of sky yet there, above him, a beam of sunshine pushed past a cloud. He smiled, stretched skywards and breathed deeply. The past was over: his older sister had left it behind and, in that moment, he determined to do the same.

At the cottage Eliza introduced him to her man, William Turner. He was a tailor from a large family of tailors and Henry immediately liked him. He was wearing a jacket, the fit of which was good. He spoke of his craft enthusiastically: as he described how he made his patterns Henry began to have an insight onto the difficulties of turning a piece of cloth into a garment that fitted around a person. It was something he had not thought about before, having dismissed tailoring as women's work. William Turner was slight of frame and his hands appeared delicate but Henry appreciated his intellect and was pleased that his sister had found a good man to support her. His happiness at her pleasure was only marred by the fact that William Turner came from Yorkshire and would take Eliza back with him after they were married.

He enjoyed the evening, especially being in Mary and Eliza's company again. They had worked together to support their father's family and they were now adults making their own way in the world. He saw his younger siblings whom he had sent away from the bad air in the cottage at Garrison

Walk. Martha was clearly well although he saw no more of her than her head as she peeped round Rachel's skirts. He tried to make conversation with Thomas, who was nine, but he did not say much. Rachel was growing up and he thought she was becoming as beautiful as her sisters. He looked back on his decision to send them away and he knew now that he had been right. Rachel was not the only young woman that Henry noticed. He was introduced to William Turner's sister, Sophia, who had accompanied him to Yarmouth. He noted the softness of her hands and the directness of her gaze: this he was very thankful for because it made it easier for him to keep his eyes from moving down her body. He imagined moving his hands down it which made his undergarments somewhat uncomfortable. The softness of her hands indicated her status: she did not work at all, either inside or outside her home. She was a young lady in the happy position of being supported by the family business. Henry's excitement quickly deflated: he was a man of no substance as he had been informed before.

Earlier that day Jim and Freddie had been turning a length of wood on the lathe to form a post. It was about eight inches longer than they needed, so, using the lathe, they formed one end into two balls. Then they removed them and smoothed the ends that had been attached to the post. Now they were in the middle of the yard throwing these for the younger ones to catch. Henry watched and Freddie, despite only having one eye, was able to catch the ball most of the time. He noticed that, as the ball approached him, he moved his head up and down rapidly.

The following morning Henry, Jim and Freddie went out to a mill on the Denes. The owner did not have a maintenance contract with them and had called them out several times the previous winter when things had gone wrong. Now he had asked for them to take on his mill and they were going to assess its condition in order to say how much it would cost to bring it up to standard. It was only then that they would put it onto a contract. They had left the town through Pudding Gate on St Nicholas's Road and were approaching the mill.

'How tall is it, Freddie?' Henry asked. Freddie flicked his head up and down a few times.

'Nearly sixty foot,' he replied.

'Well I agree with that. I'm interested in how you do it because when I was a boy I would sometimes close one eye when I was looking at things and my father told me to stop. He said I must not become used to closing one eye because, as a millwright, I would need two to judge distances. But you seem to manage?'

Freddie laughed. 'Yes, and I've noticed you watching me.' Freddie moved his head up and down and Henry smiled as he continued. 'I think I learnt how to do it when I was playing in the sand dunes as a boy but I can't remember how I worked it out – it just happened. I think I didn't fall as much when I jumped if I moved my head. I didn't know at the time that I was judging distances – and sometimes I was called Noddy!' He shrugged. 'I might have felt somewhat peevish at first, especially when they called me names, but I soon realised it was something that I had to do because of my eye – and, in any case, I couldn't stop myself. But then, the nickname didn't stick.'

'Probably because it doesn't fit,' said Henry, 'you only nod your head, you're not stupid!'

'And because you laughed about it as well,' said Jim. 'I can remember Edmund being disgruntled because he and his cronies couldn't upset you when you first came up from junior boys. It was the same as when you had your first day at the yard - you just ignored him and he couldn't understand that because he knew that if someone called him names he didn't like it.'

'Oh, I didn't care for it much either,' laughed Freddie, 'but I wasn't showing him that - or anyone else.' They arrived at the mill and Henry set them to work with a list of things to check whilst he stayed outside to look at the condition of the sails. He missed his brother William but he was very glad to have the company of Jim and Freddie: they both had a ready wit and laughed a lot so that, even on the days when Henry woke up sad, he didn't stay that way after he reached the yard.

14

Since the expansion of their silkworks Grout's had built houses for their workers near the factory. They complained that Pudding Gate on St Nicholas road cut them off from the rest of the town and the traffic through the gate had started to form queues making it difficult for them to transport the finished silk to the docks on South Quay. It was decided that Pudding Gate would be demolished and St Nicholas's Road widened. A few weeks before this happened Henry went up the square tower that surrounded the gate and looked out on the town. He could remember, as a small boy coming with his grandfather, Thomas, who had begun the family business, and he wondered what his grandfather would have made of the many buildings that he could see. Thomas had talked about a time before Henry was born when building outside the walls was not allowed. As he looked he realised that soon the town would be as big outside the walls as inside. He turned to look over St Nicholas's graveyard in the direction of Caister. Beyond the houses along Caister Road, one of which his Uncle James and family inhabited, he could see what he thought were other houses being built.

'I see they're building again – along Caister Road beyond your house?' Henry asked James a few days later at the yard.

'A new workhouse,' he replied. Henry raised his eyebrows.

His uncle continued, 'Apparently the old one is not big enough, especially now that the able-bodied will not receive out-relief.'

Henry frowned. 'Then they are expected to go into the workhouse? Or starve?'

'They have to find work, any work, even if it is not what they usually do.'

'What, you mean…'

James nodded, 'Anything. That means if you lost your work today, tomorrow you could be shovelling muck from the privies.'

Henry pulled a face. 'So there's no more out-relief to tide you over until you find work with your skills.'

'That's right. They are going to need room for many more people – the families of the men as well. Those are the rules that the government have put in place – if you can work, you must, or go into the workhouse.'

'Great Yarmouth has always treated the poor well. For example, in this town there are many who have work when the herrings are in but then are laid off until next time. They are not idle, just unfortunate.'

'Well, perhaps they'll be more lenient with the rules here, but in any case, there will be a need for a bigger workhouse and it's being built just along from my house. I may move. It's a pity, I don't like the hardheartedness of it all. As a family we have always looked after those less well off than ourselves. My Hannah, with your Ma and Robert's Mary, often went visiting poor families. It's the children that suffer in hard times and in the workhouse they'd be separated from their parents.'

'Mind, we both know families where the man could work and doesn't – and then receives the out-relief and spends it on ale – in the same way as others do their wages.'

'Yes, the lazy will always be here,' said James. His eyes flicked over to Edmund and Henry noticed. He shrugged at the unfairness of life but did not comment.

Later that morning Henry was on his way out to another water-pump with his apprentices Jim and Freddie. They passed the building site.

'Your father was telling me that this is going to be a new workhouse.'

'Yes,' nodded Freddie. He frowned and Henry couldn't help smiling. Freddie's frown caused the scar that covered his left eye socket to move onto his forehead and, with his mouth pulled up into a permanent half-grin by the skin of his face as it had healed after the hot coals had landed on it when he was a baby, the effect was clown-like. Freddie caught sight of the smile and groaned. 'I can't be serious even when I try,' he laughed. 'The workhouse – we were discussing it last night. This new system – I think it's good that those who look on out-relief as a reason not to work, even though they can, should not receive it. If they are placed somewhere where they have to work and where they're separated from their families and the food is adequate but unappetising, perhaps working for their living will be attractive.'

'What of those who cannot work?' responded Henry.

'And what of their wives and children? Should they be punished because the men are lazy?' added Jim.

'Yes, I agree that each person needs careful scrutiny and Pa was saying that he thought that Yarmouth Board would show compassion.' Then he pointed to his face. 'But I could say, "Pity me!". It has always made people treat me unkindly, especially when I was younger.'

Jim nodded, 'I can remember defending you many times!'

'Yes, I once refused to go to school. Pa let me stay at home that day but when he returned from work we went out for a long walk together and I never stayed at home again. There was another boy at school, Alfred I think, who dragged one leg as he walked. I know he doesn't work now but stays at home with his Ma. If something happens to his Pa then I can see he and his Ma looking for relief. A while in the workhouse may give him the courage to face a few taunts at work! You wondered if I could work at this craft with one eye but I can because I've learnt how.'

'We agreed last night that something else ought to be done for the women and children,' explained Jim to Henry, 'perhaps allowing very young children to be with their mothers and a workhouse school for the older ones.'

Henry nodded. 'Those who are poor are a difficult problem.' He paused, remembering the years at Garrison Walk and how he'd almost put his parents in the workhouse. 'But then not everyone who falls on hard times is at fault.' The pitch of his voice changed as resentment towards his father suddenly welled up inside him, taking him unawares: he'd scarcely thought of him for months.

'You have overcome great difficulties,' Jim pointed out. 'Pa told us,' he explained at Henry's look of surprise. Henry looked at his two apprentices. Freddie clapped him on the back.

'We think you're wonderful.' They were both grinning now and Henry could not help but smile: his angst faded as quickly as it had appeared.

'Now – to work,' he said as they approached the pump they had come to repair.

May arrived and spirits were high in Yarmouth. There was a new queen in London and she would be crowned in June. There had not been a queen on the throne for over a hundred years and throughout the country men in ale houses discussed the phenomenon. It would be a time of festivity and people looked forward to having fun and forgetting, for a day, their usual, often dreary, lives. The town corporation had announced that they would be organising celebrations that would include everyone in the town, whatever their class. Almost every week there was a proclamation from the bellman about another event that would be happening after which he would pin a notice to the door of the Angel in Market Place.

'I was talking to Mr Hall, the blacksmith, in the King's Arms last night,' announced Robert one morning at the yard. Everyone looked up from where they were working. 'He has thrown down a challenge, a race that this year will happen as part of the coronation celebrations on the Denes.' Edmund looked horrified but the others grinned because they had been defeated by Hall's the previous summer and now relished the possibility of regaining their honour. Last year one apprentice from each yard was chosen by lot and when Edmund drew the cross for Spandler's all the other apprentices had groaned. They knew that Spandler's would lose especially when they saw the challenge: a sack was placed at the feet of the two apprentices whom the lot had chosen, in which was a fifty-yard chain with a thickness of a man's wrist. Each apprentice had to find the end of the chain and then lift it, link by heavy link, over his head so that it ended up in a pile behind him. Edmund had had beads of sweat on his forehead before the start and didn't even manage to move half of the chain before he gave up.

'What have we to do this year?' asked Freddie.

'You'll be pleased to know that we have free choice as to which apprentices represent us.' Everyone cheered and Edmund let out the breath he had been holding. 'Both yards have to bring an object, weighing not less than half a ton, which four apprentices will carry from the windmills near the silk factory to the sea, the winner being the first team to drop their object in the water with a splash.'

'Half a ton,' Jim, Freddie's brother, paused, wrinkling his brow as he thought. 'I should say that a length of stout tree trunk about three or four feet long would be right. Are we allowed to attach handles?'

'Yes, as long as the object weighs more than half a ton we can do what we want. Mr Greensome from the nursery has agreed to provide scales – he's organising a race that will need them – something to do with potatoes – so our weights will be checked before we set off.'

The following morning, as the men were standing around Bessie with their tea, they discussed their plans.

'I think we need to make sure that our weight is as heavy as it has to be but no heavier,' someone suggested.

'Yes,' agreed Freddie.

'You asked about handles yesterday,' Edmund pointed out, 'but that will make it heavier than it needs to be.' He eyed the other apprentices and some of them nodded hesitantly as if they were agreeing with him but then a voice at the back called out.

'How do you think we're going to carry it without handles Ed? Use the branches?' A few of the apprentices smiled.

'I thought you would carry it on your shoulders,' he replied, a defensive edge audible in his voice.

'So, you don't want to be part of our team then? You're not offering to carry it?' Edmund paled as everyone laughed. Jim, Freddie's brother, came to his side.

'Don't be too hard on him. He could be involved in the design.' There were a few murmurs but no-one objected and Jim continued. He spoke to everyone but was careful to catch Edmund's eyes as he spoke. Henry, who was watching, hoped that the kindness was appreciated. 'I have thought about it overnight. We must weigh a length of trunk and the rope which we'll use to make the handles - together they need to be more than half a ton. Then we can put holes through the bottom third of the trunk and grooves down the sides, feed the rope through the holes and splice it to create handles which then cannot be pulled out of the holes. That way we can claim that the handles are part of the object. If we weigh it again after we've attached the handles we can work out how much to shave off the ends to make it exactly half a ton.'

'That's a lot of work,' said Freddie. 'Perhaps we should just try it on our shoulders first.' He looked at Edmund who beamed at the support and looked around the yard.

'There's a length over there. Too small probably but we could try,' Edmund suggested. 'I would not be much good in the race but I'm willing to try it now with some of you.' There were murmurs of surprise from the other apprentices. Edmund looked up and caught Henry's eye. Henry smiled and nodded.

'Well done, Ed,' Jim said quietly to him whilst Freddie also smiled. Edmund looked from one to the other of his cousins and grinned. He was perspiring heavily by the time they had carried the wood a few yards.

'That didn't work,' he announced, although they had all seen how they bumped up against each other as they moved: in a race each man would stop the other from moving quickly. Some of the men raised their eyes and smirked behind his back but changed their countenance when Henry looked at them.

After the holes had been drilled the following week the handles needed to be made: this involved splicing the rope as closely as possible to the holes which had been drilled in the log. Splicing was a skill all the men had to acquire as part of their training but no-one liked doing it: pulling the strands of the rope apart enough to enable the ends to be woven into the rope would rub their fingers, which were often chapped and sore from working outside in the wet, so that they bled. Hence when Edmund offered to do it some of them expressed surprise. They all kept glancing at him as they worked at other tasks and saw that Edmund's podgy fingers were surprising strong and agile. Henry disliked his cousin and found him to be untrustworthy but he realised he was not well and acknowledged that on this occasion he was trying to play his part in the working of the millwrights' yard. He was first in line to become the master millwright in charge upon the demise of his father, a role for which Henry doubted he would have the ability to fulfil. However, Edmund had surprised him that   afternoon.

15

Thursday the twenty-eighth of June 1838, the day of the Queen's coronation, dawned fine and, in London, it stayed that way for the whole day. However, in Yarmouth, the clouds started to gather as the sun left its zenith and, although the boat race was completed with scarcely a wind, by three o'clock it was raining. Because the rain had firmed up the sands, the horse races continued, and several thousand people stayed to watch. As they finished Edmund Hall and Robert Spandler spoke with Mr Simpson, the gentleman who was organising the races. He turned to the crowds and shouted that the blacksmiths and the millwrights would now race. A few people had started to leave but turned back: whilst a coronation happened but rarely, the challenges were an annual entertainment and the rivalry between the two families was well known.

Henry went to stand with his uncles, Robert and James, whilst four of their apprentices went to the tree trunk and took hold of the handles. A few feet away from them four of Hall's apprentices lifted a lump of iron. There was much cheering from the crowd as they heaved their weights towards the sea. Mr Simpson had had the presence of mind to appoint two young men as umpires and they ran alongside the teams. Robert, James and Henry stood tall to try and see but from where they were it was impossible to judge which weight splashed into the sea first. Then the umpires turned to the crowds and lifted the arms of the Spandler apprentices. Robert and James grinned and Henry leapt into the air. They were about to go to join their team when Mr Simpson blew his whistle.

'Spandler's are victorious,' he shouted and the crowd cheered again. It was raining quite heavily by now and when he looked at the small group of gentlemen who were standing nearby they nodded and he continued, 'the rest of the races will take place at three of the clock tomorrow afternoon when, God willing, the sun will shine.'

By the time Robert, James and Henry reached the apprentices they were already part of the way up the beach.

'We'll take that back to the yard. You've done well this afternoon. When you reach the yard you'll find some ale there and my good wife has been to the bakers this morning.'

Half an hour later Robert, James and Henry heaved the wood through the door of the yard. They took one look at the scene before them, clunked the wood down onto the floor and looked at each other in amazement.

Edmund was serving the other apprentices.

Freddie grinned. 'He didn't want to but we said that as we'd won the prize and he didn't even bother to come and cheer us on, then he ought to be our servant.'

Robert laughed, 'Well done son,' he slapped Edmund on the back, 'but how did you make him do it?' he asked Freddie.

'Told him it was that or we'd duck him in the water barrel!' Everyone laughed while Edmund scowled.

'It's unjust,' he bleated, 'I am not well.'

When all the families of the men arrived to join the celebrations the other apprentices told Edmund that they would not insist that he waited on everybody. Edmund took that to mean he could stop altogether and, as Henry noticed that his skin was paler than usual and his lips were dark, he was prepared to intervene should anyone try to make him continue – but then Henry observed that his ill-health did not prevent him moving his large frame back and forth between his seat and the food table!

However he soon forgot about Edmund because his sisters and brothers arrived. He watched while Freddie entertained Tom and the younger ones by wiggling his scars and pulling strange faces. After they'd finished laughing Freddie lectured them on the foolishness of coming too close to the fire. Henry enjoyed being with them and looked forward to the next day when the celebrations would continue.

The following afternoon Eliza and Mary, with Rachel, Tom and Martha, met Henry at the yard and they all walked down St Nicholas's Road. They emerged onto the Denes and looked along the shore. There were crowds of people as far as they could see. They could hear music from both ends of the sands as two brass bands played. Shouts and laughter filled the air and Tom and Martha jumped up and down in excitement.

'Where shall we go?' Rachel asked Henry.

'You and I can take Thomas and Martha and find a good place from where to watch the races and other entertainment.' He turned to Mary and Eliza and gave them a sixpence. 'And while we're doing that you could buy us all some food.'

'A whole tanner – a feast you mean?' Eliza's eyes danced with glee.

Henry laughed. 'Well, buy plenty, we don't want to be hungry!'

The Denes, where tough grasses had taken a hold, gave way to the sand of the beach. A stage had been built on the beach and an area of the Denes had been designated as the stands. Mary was smiling as she watched where Henry and Rachel went. Meanwhile Eliza had seen the stall belonging to Boulter's the bakers and quickly joined the queue.

'Good afternoon,' said Mr Boulter, smiling in recognition as she approached. Boulter's had their premises on North Road directly opposite Spandler's yard and the two families knew each other.

'Good afternoon,' she replied. 'A large loaf. Can you split the crust, please?' Charles Boulter nodded as Eliza continued, 'and I'll have half a dozen of your farthing currant buns as well.' She licked her lips in anticipation of the sweetness as she placed them in her basket. From the basket she took a large glass bottle to another stall where, for a penny, it was filled with a liquor containing lemons and sugar known as lemonade.

Small fires, many of them, had been lit along the sands. On the fires food, mostly fish, was being cooked. Eliza bought ten plump herrings and put them into the slit in the loaf where any of the oil which oozed from the warm fish would be absorbed by the bread. The two young women walked to where Mary had seen the others disappear from sight. For a few moments they could not see them until Eliza caught sight of Thomas who was still jumping up and down.

'There they are,' she said. 'I think Tom saw us. He could tell that we didn't know where they were.'

Mary laughed. 'And he was worried that we might just sit down and eat all the fish ourselves!'

Thomas was still agitated when they reached them.

'Calm down now, Tom,' Rachel said. 'Have you removed the sand from your fingers?' Thomas clapped his hands together.

'And keep them off the sand while you're eating,' suggested Henry, 'that's unless you like sand with your herring. Once you have fish oil on your fingers, if you touch the sand, you can clap all you like but you'll never get it off.' Eliza pulled the bread apart to share it between them and gave them each some fish as well. As Henry finished he made a loud slurp as he removed the last of the fish from his fingers. Everyone laughed.

'It's just as well Uncle Robert and Aunt Mary are not with us,' said Thomas, 'because she does not like it if you make a noise when you eat. That's unless you're called Edmund. He made a noise at dinner the other night and I was blamed and made to leave the table.'

No-one noticed Tom's comment as people around them fell quiet: Mr Simpson had climbed onto the stage to announce the first race and they all turned to see what was happening. Mary gave everyone a currant bun while they watched. Mr Simpson was supervising two men as they struggled to lift a huge tub onto the stage into which they emptied the contents of two large flour sacks. Just after they started pouring Mr Simpson stopped them and pulled, with a flourish, two florins from his pocket. The air filled with oohs and cheers. He put them in the tub and the men recommenced pouring the flour. As it was being poured Mr Simpson also added a handful of pennies accompanied by more clapping and cheering.

'Apprentices from Walker's the chimney sweeps!' Mr Simpson announced, as two youths, their faces and clothes black with soot, filed onto the stage and stood either side of the tub. Mr Simpson clapped his hands and the boys, holding onto the sides of the tub, dived their heads into the flour. They both shot back up again, yelped, rubbed their heads and sneezed. The crowd roared with laughter!

'Look at them,' someone shouted, 'black at the bottom and white at the top!' By the time they had finished both Mary and Eliza were wiping tears from their eyes.

'I've not laughed so much for a long time,' said Mary. Henry nodded in agreement, his own eyes twinkling. He looked with pleasure at his brothers and sisters and, although he was sad when he remembered about the others who had died, there were six of them here, his father's family, happy and healthy: he was no longer wracked by guilt.

This was followed by boys from Greensome's nursery, bobbing for oranges in a tub of water. The oranges had been donated by the captain of a ship which had docked on South Quay earlier that week. Next came a singing competition, won by an urchin, poorly dressed: he did not have the best singing voice but he performed with comedy enough to set the crowd laughing again.

The men on the stage were now carrying on a long table which they covered with a chequered tablecloth.

'The tea drinkers of Yarmouth,' announced Mr Simpson. With some considerable difficulty six elderly women climbed onto the platform.

'Where did they find those old crones?' shouted someone from the crowd. The women were un-abashed by the comments and laughter that greeted them as they walked up and down the stage, smiling and waving. The men brought chairs onto the stage and placed them behind the table and the women immediately scurried to their seats. A large teacup was placed in front of each one. Sugar bowls appeared and all six grinned and nodded their heads, firstly at each other and then at the audience before quickly helping themselves to many spoonsful of sugar. Two maids came onto the stage with large teapots and proceeded to pour the tea.

When the tea is poured they can start to drink,' announced Mr Simpson. 'The first with an empty cup will receive a sovereign.' Shouting and cheering erupted from the crowd.

'Look at the poor old dears,' said Mary as the ladies slurped the tea. 'It's so hot and they are trying to drink it as quickly as they can.'

'They're enjoying themselves!' exclaimed Henry.

'But look at the faces they're pulling when they take a large mouthful.' Mary's hand was on her own mouth. 'It's hurting them!'

Rachel pointed at the ladies on the stage. 'It's alright – now they're laughing and waving at the crowd again.' The women had finished their tea and were walking to the edge of the stage to be helped down – all except the one who won the sovereign. She went to the edge of the stage as if she was going to get down but then walked round and round the table, taking another bow each time. The crowd cheered! Eventually Mr Simpson went and took her arm. She smiled, looked at him and nodded in approval. It was not often she walked with a gentleman: she shortened her stride and tried to walk like a lady but the effect was quite comical. She momentarily stopped and frowned at the laughter before standing as tall as the curvature of her spine would accommodate and allowing

Mr Simpson to escort her from the stage waving at the crowd as she went.

'I'm sure you are all thirsty after that, so the committee has provided ale,' Mr Simpson announced. The crowd cheered at this announcement as he continued, 'There are twenty-four barrels being dispensed all over the Denes.'

Henry took a large cup from Eliza's basket and went to join one of the queues whilst the girls shared the lemonade.

'The pig-catching was funny,' said Rachel as they left the Denes later that afternoon.

'They squealed but still managed to get away,' said Martha.

'That's because there was soap on their tales,' laughed Tom, 'and I couldn't stop laughing at the old men gingling.'

'Is that what you call it when they pull those funny faces with their heads stuck through horse collars?' asked Martha.

'Yes,' replied Tom, 'but if I pulled faces like that I would be told I was childish.'

'That's because you would be!' exclaimed Henry, but Tom could see that Henry was teasing him and they both laughed. By this point they were walking up St Nicholas's road. Because the middle of the road had been churned up since the heavy rain the day before they walked near to the houses and Tom and Henry were walking together.

'How old are you now?' Henry asked, 'when will you leave school and start at the yard?'

'I'm only ten,' Henry looked surprised and Tom continued, 'and yes, I know, everyone tells me I look older. Uncle Robert says I look as if I'm old enough to earn some money but I won't be leaving school just yet.'

Henry shrugged. 'You're not really a child any more. In a few years it will be time you paid your way.'

'I-I-I don't want to work at the yard.'

'I don't understand,' said Henry. 'Why not?'

'Because I don't want to work with Edmund. It's bad enough at the cottage after school. Anything that he breaks, any task that he doesn't do, he blames on me.'

'But it's the Spandler family business!' Henry's eyebrows raised and his eyes stared.

Tom stood still. 'It's their business. I know it's theirs, not ours at all.' He met his elder brother's gaze. Henry broke eye contact and walked on for another twenty paces in silence. When he spoke he did so through lips that were barely open.

'How do you know?'

'Because Ed never stops reminding me of it.' Henry bit his bottom lip as Tom continued, 'says my part of the Spandler family have squandered their position which makes me a person of no importance. He's asked me a few times if I know why you're still here. I don't think he likes you much – but it might be something to do with his father who keeps saying how proficient you are.'

'Well I'm glad that I annoy him by my presence,' replied Henry with a short laugh. 'If I'd been thinking of leaving Yarmouth, I probably wouldn't now that you have told me that! And it's good to know that Uncle Robert thinks highly of me.' Tom did not say anything else. His shoulders drooped but Henry failed to notice. In the coming months Henry would look back on the conversation and regret that he didn't talk to Tom more but his head was full of the thought that Robert valued him and that that annoyed Edmund. It made him smile.

They had reached the top of St Nicholas's Road and walked together along North road. Outside the door to Spandler's yard they split up. Eliza, Tom and Martha went into the yard to the cottage where they lived with Robert and his family while Mary and Rachel went to Hannah's. Henry continued alone into Rampart Row, the gloom wiping the smile from his face. His sense of outrage at Edmund's privileges darkened his mind obscuring any thoughts about Tom. He looked forward to the ale he would drink at Maria's.

Summer turned to autumn and as the nights drew in conversations at the yard turned to the weather and the winter to come. Amongst members of the family questions started to be asked about Christmas: it was a special time for the Spandlers when, for a few days, the yard stopped and was transformed by evergreens and berries into a place for midwinter celebrations. Henry didn't know whether his grandfather had begun the tradition after he bought the yard, or even if the family came together before that, because all he knew was that as long as he could remember there were these few days when there was no work done: when he was a child he noticed that the adults were different and he and his cousins giggled together, saying that they were drunk. Now he knew that, although plenty of ale was supped, it was the change in routine and the suspension of work that caused the jollity. A lot of planning and preparation meant that for a few days even the women of the family had not too much to do and could relax. This year Henry's thoughts of Christmas were tinged with sadness because the date for Eliza's marriage to William had been set at the twenty-ninth of December. Soon she would leave Yarmouth. Eliza was his sibling and his father had charged him with her care when he had gone to London even though she was older than him by two years. She was alive, and he could count her as one of the successes in contrast to the others who were dead, but Yorkshire was so far away he doubted that he would ever see her again. She had been his support. The fact that she was one of his father's children who was taking her place in the world gave him some satisfaction. However, it did not make him happy.

His father had disinherited him. He enjoyed his work and knew he was good at it but he would never have the satisfaction of being the master-in-charge and running the yard. Instead he would have to watch his cousin inherit what should have been his position and see him destroy the yard by his ineptitude.

38842908R00075

Printed in Poland
by Amazon Fulfillment
Poland Sp. z o.o., Wrocław